The Power of Nothingness

The Power of

*Other books by Alexandra David-Neel
and Lama Yongden*

Mipam, Le Lama aux Cinq Sagesses

Magie d'Amour et Magie Noire

Boston
1982

Nothingness

Alexandra David-Neel *and* Lama Yongden

Translated and with an Introduction by
Janwillem van de Wetering

Houghton Mifflin Company

Library of Congress Cataloging in Publication Data

David-Neel, Alexandra, 1868–1969.
The power of nothingness.

Translation of: La puissance du néant.
I. Yongden, Albert Arthur. II. Title.
PQ2607.A927P813 1982   843'.912   81-23737
ISBN 0-395-31557-3   AACR2

they rise from the mind
and extinguish themselves into the mind

Milarepa

Introduction

ALEXANDRA DAVID-NEEL was born in Paris in 1868. She died in Digne (France) one hundred years later. A century is a ripe old age for a human being, but it isn't an impossible age. Madame David-Neel perpetrated, however, the impossible.

She originated from acceptable stock: her father was French, and a Huguenot; her mother came from Scandinavia and professed the Catholic faith. Alexandra read Jules Verne in defense. At age 15 she ran away to England, with a raincoat and a philosophy book in the way of baggage. She was found and sent home. At age 17, similarly equipped, she improved her record. This time she walked through Switzerland by way of the St. Gotthard and discovered the Italian lakes. She really liked the lakes and told her parents, by postcard. Her mother found her a little later, in Milano. The girl was persuaded to return to Paris, but some promises were required. Certainly, Alexandra would be allowed to study philosophy and, why not, Eastern languages. The year was 1885. The professors at the College de France demurred but the young lady, having traveled, knew that obstacles can be removed if their illusionary nature is realized. She brought some paper and a pencil and sat down in the back of the class. The professors fussed. Alexandra paid no attention.

The professors taught. Alexandra paid a lot of attention, especially when she discovered that at least one of them seemed to know what he was talking about. Professor Eduard Foucaux, mentioned in several of Madame David-Neel's books, taught Tibetan history, culture, and language.

Tibet, in those days, was a land of mystic mystery, a country of mountains that dwarfed the European Alps, interspersed by desolate plains. It was ruled by a priestly king, the Dalai Lama, its state religion was Buddhism, and it kept its formidable natural frontiers closed. Several of the currently powerful countries had their eyes on the strategic region, but only China managed to invade "the roof of the world," although not too successfully. The Tibetan guerrillas knew how to appear and disappear, and the Chinese soldiers hardly ever survived their brief visits. They also froze and starved to death because neither equipment nor food could reach them. Tibet had no roads, only trails, too narrow for wheeled transport, a novelty the country didn't believe in. Wheels were only used for prayer. A monk who didn't feel like reciting the Buddha's teaching could insert the written text in a receptacle attached to a wheel. Spin the wheel and the holy words were endlessly reproduced, emitted silently, to spread their benevolent message in all directions. But wheels trundling along a road, carrying carts loaded with passengers and goods — no. The sturdy, smiling population felt more comfortable riding horses and mules, and goods traveled on the backs of yaks. Yaks are slow, but the country knew no haste. Only foreigners hurry: the slender, sly Chinese, for instance, and the exotic but equally despicable white-skinned, blue-eyed demons from the West.

Alexandra finished her studies, married an Englishman, and decided that she wanted to see Tibet. Mr. David-Neel, who must have been an understanding type, was told that she would be away for only a year and a half. He corresponded with her — from his London rooms — for 13 years, then she came back and immediately left again. Little is known about the gentleman but Alexandra's French publishers claim that he was quiet and polite. When Mrs. David-Neel eventually retired in France she had spent 30 years in the Far East and her husband had died.

In 1910 (she was 42 then and traveling about in India, where she studied local lore), she heard that the Dalai Lama had left Lhasa to avoid being captured by the Chinese and was residing in Madras. Madame David-Neel was told that the god-king refused to see European ladies, but she presented some letters of introduction, signed by high Indian dignitaries, that informed His Holiness that the prospective visitor was a practicing Buddhist, knowledgeable, fluent in his language, free of greed, and definitely not a spy.

The supreme priest and temporarily deposed ruler invited the exceptional supplicant to his court, where Alexandra was impressed by her host's personality and the character of his retainers: tall men dressed in dark red robes, yellow satin coats, and brocade vests. She felt that the country these men represented harbored secrets of extraordinary value. Difficulties prevailed, however, and the lady had to exercise patience. She stayed close to the refugees and perfected her knowledge of the language. Then, in 1912, she crossed the frontier, at that time controlled by the Chinese.

After a slow ascent, she was awed by the mauve and orange snowcapped mountains, which maintained an eternity of such unbelievable splendor that she was certain at first that the arduous journey had made her hallucinate.

The experience surpassed everything Asia had given her so far. Soon she would receive gifts of another order. She began to collect original Buddhist texts, sought out literate lamas, and interviewed hermit-adepts living in caves.

Alexandra David-Neel was the first female traveler to

penetrate the Tibetan mystery. The European males who preceded her had been few and were either motivated by national or personal greed or the urge to spread the Christian faith. Jesuits reached Lhasa early in the eighteenth century but as neither their creed nor their method appealed to their hosts they were forced to leave. A Dutch adventurer, Van der Putte, managed to become the Dalai Lama's guest at the monastery called Potala, the country's spiritual and governmental seat. He arrived in 1720 and left two years later. French missionaries established a short-lived station in 1860 and British army officers began to snoop about a little later. They eventually called in reinforcements that were attacked by Tibetan irregular troops. The British army, under Youngfellow, shelled Lhasa in retaliation. A victory was proclaimed but the expedition, short of supplies and uncertain about what it was trying to achieve, retreated to India. The Chinese Imperial Army took its place and even occupied Lhasa, but Peking was torn by internal strife and morale was low. Tibetan herdsmen rallied under tough chiefs and drove the invaders out. By then the Tibetans had made up their minds; they wanted nothing to do with any foreigners and closed their borders hermetically. The Dalai Lama was back in his mountain fortress and his rule of self-sufficiency was strictly enforced. Alexandra, who had managed to journey into the borderlands, claimed vainly that her motives were pure, but was told to leave, together with the fleeing Chinese soldiers.

She traveled elsewhere, mostly in India, but couldn't forget the glimpse she had been granted. She tried once again to obtain a visa, in her semiofficial capacity as linguist and student of Eastern religions, sponsored by dignitaries in India and Europe. The border guards, picturesquely attired in long robes and carrying outdated but deadly arms, refused to listen to her request. When she came back the next day the guards never noticed her for she had dressed up as a local woman and shuffled past their forbidding forms bent double under a load of hay. Who would pay notice to a poor female, wrapped up in tattered coats and scarfs, mumbling polite greetings? Alexandra made sure that the guards didn't see her face for the Tibetans believe that only demons have blue eyes, and demons were unpopular in the holy Buddhist land. She didn't go far on the first leap of the journey she had prepared for so long but waited at the first opportune spot for a caravan of seven heavily loaded mules that followed her under the expert guidance of a Tibetan lama, Yongden. She had met Yongden, a spiritually talented young man of elevated rank (*lama* means adept or teacher), a few years earlier in India, where he had helped her to perfect her knowledge of the Tibetan language and promised to assist in her forbidden search.

This was the first of a number of lengthy journeys that would give the author the opportunity to acquaint herself thoroughly with a rare and profound culture. She lived in monasteries and hermitages and was taught the secret rites of Tantric Buddhism. She meditated. She learned how to make *mantras* (holy sayings) and *yantras* (holy charts) divulge their inner meanings. She passed initiations and became a lama herself. She wrote at least 20 books, some easy to read like the best-sellers *A Parisienne's Journey to Lhasa* and *Magic and Mystery in Tibet*, both translated into English, and some on Buddhist teaching, reprinted several times in France. She also wrote a Tibetan grammar and several scholarly works on India and China. She never thought of writing a novel until she returned to France.

Her adopted son, faithful companion, teacher, and disciple, the lama Yongden (who died in France in 1955), was irritated at times by the nonsensical books written on Tibet by amateur Europeans and Americans who grossly misinterpreted the scant information they might have acquired.

"Write something yourself," Madame David-Neel said.

"Here you are," the lama replied.

He gave her the manuscript of the first Tibetan novel, set in a contemporary background. She studied his attempt and rewrote it in French, giving him credit for creating its plot, characters, and general outline. It was published, in both French and English, as *Mipam*, subtitled *The Lama of the Five Wisdoms*. Good sales and reviews encouraged the co-authors, and second and third novels appeared: *La Puissance du Néant* and *Magie d'Amour et Magie Noire*.

*

As a boy I liked to browse in the bookstores of my native Rotterdam. A helpful assistant, wanting to get rid of an item that had been gathering dust, showed me a Dutch translation of *Mipam*. I opened it at random and read a passage. The translator, no doubt a very old lady who liked archaic Dutch, used words I had never heard of. I gathered the book had to do with Tibet and remembered that my geography teacher had described the country as the most mysterious on earth. I bought the novel, made an effort to make some sense out of its dense language, gasped, and stayed up most of the night. I had found what I had been looking for for some time: a tale involving human beings living completely unlike anybody I knew. Pure science fiction and therefore neither scientific nor fictional. Place: this planet. Time: about right now.

I immediately read the book again and heard about magic that really worked, predestination, reincarnation, karma, necromancers, and saints. I was given hidden hints at truths that I vaguely recognized. Good and evil were explained in an entirely different way, more intelligently it seemed than in the dazzling-white/pitch-black doctrine dominating Holland at that time. And right through the whole story, which contained enough straight adventure to keep me bright-eyed,

I saw a thread of cynical humor and realism holding both plot and the credibility of the hero down to solid ground. I reread this version of *Mipam* many times and had it bound in leather when it finally fell apart. Some years later I learned enough French to be able to read the original but couldn't find a copy.

Then, last year, a recent French reprint of Mrs. David-Neel's first novel found me, in the offices of a Boston publisher, Houghton Mifflin. I promptly went berserk, rushed into the office of my editor, and demanded to know where he got it. He didn't remember. He receives books every day, many of which float around the premises until they get lost.

"Take it," he said. "Keep it. And don't flap your arms."

I spent the rest of the day reading in a nearby café. I went back to the editor and told him to give me a contract, there and then, to translate *Mipam* into English.

"No."

"Why not?"

"Because it's available in English."

I wouldn't leave and insisted on telling him all that I knew about Madame David-Neel. He yawned politely and told me that he had looked the lady up. *A Parisienne's Journey to Lasa* had indeed been a best-seller, in 1927. "A bit outdated now, don't you think?"

"*What?*" I shouted. "Never! Tibet may be incorporated with China now, but its spirit pervades the West. The lamas are right here, in Boulder, Colorado, in New York, in Boston!"

"*You* are in Boston," he said. "Staying long?"

Never underestimate editors. He took his time but finally sent me the copy of Mrs. David-Neel's and Lama Yongden's second novel, *La Puissance du Néant*. I stopped all other activity and read it four times. Then I phoned Boston.

"Well?"

"Better," I said. "Even better than the first. This one is a thriller. It has all the elements: a murder, a criminal, a private eye. And it's written the other way around, like some of the modern mysteries that are popular now. You find out who has done it at once and then follow the detective."

"Does he catch the villain in the end?"

"Never mind. Nothing to do with you."

"No?"

"No."

"Anything else in it?"

"Some. Tibet is in it. A hermit in a cave. Assorted demons, real ones, not the blue-eyed variety from the West. A turquoise the size of an egg. Taoism. Pigs, not real pigs but police pigs. A desert. Big Mongolian camels. A successful businessman diminishing his capital. Wolves. A good chase. A sensuous young widow. A Zen master."

"What? I thought you were talking about Tibet."

"Yes, but the detective travels. So the reader can witness a confrontation between a Tantric guru and a Zen master. They agree fundamentally, although technically one of them is dead."

"Enlightenment?"

"Naturally."

"What do you know about enlightenment?"

"Nothing."

"What did Alexandra know about it?"

"Something, she graduated from the monastery of Kum Bum."

He laughed. "Right. I'll let you know. Hang up now, this call is costing you money."

So he wrote and commissioned the translation, which included, I'm sorry to say, some rewriting. Madame David-Neel tends to repeat herself and the modern reader may object to reading similar passages in successive chapters. I also incorporated her footnotes into the text to make the information more lively. It was a pleasure to work on this book and I hope I'll have a chance to translate the final novel in the series: *Magie d'Amour et Magie Noire*. If *Mipam* is classified as "adventure," *The Power of Nothingness* becomes "a novel of suspense." The third book is pure horror. There are some scenes in that book . . . but let's not rush ahead.

*

You may want to know what happened to Alexandra when, at age 76, she stopped traveling and writing. I quote from the obituary in the *International Herald Tribune*, published in Paris, September 9, 1969: *"Mrs. David-Neel shut herself away for the last 24 years in a secluded southern villa, crammed with Buddhist statues, masks, and prayer wheels."*

Her ashes, together with those of Lama Yongden, were taken to India and scattered, according to her wishes, in the Ganges. The source of that venerable river lies in Alexandra's beloved Tibet. A land that, as Lama Chögyam Trungpa, head of Naropa Institute in Boulder, Colorado, says, "is geographically dead" but very much with us today.

JANWILLEM VAN DE WETERING

The Power of Nothingness

1 A LONE MAN carrying a bag hurries across the immense emptiness of the Chang Tang, the plains of northern Tibet. Night is falling. Around the traveler darkness increases and envelops him insidiously with a kind of persistent aggression. The isolated rocks, wrinkles of the mountains, take on unexpected and frightening forms; the pale green eyes of the lakes embedded in the grasslands spy on the nocturnal sorcery. It's the hour when the hosts of evil spirits leave their hiding places and roam about in search of prey.

Fear creeps up and grows along with the darkness. The solitary man trembles, he has lingered too long. Panting, he hurries on.

*

Far away a horseman gallops with slanted reins, overcome by an overwhelming terror that renders him insensible to the gloom of the darkening wilderness.

Phantoms, both of them, activated by mysterious threads on the roof of the world.

*

Meanwhile, the man carrying the bag has reached his goal: the foot of a slope split in the middle by a cave that has been primitively equipped to serve as a hermitage.

This hermitage belonged to a guru, the teacher of Munpa Des-song and several other disciples. But while, as a special favor, Munpa had been permitted to live close to the cave so that he could serve the guru as his attendant, his co-disciples had to content themselves with short stays in the vicinity for training periods whose duration the teacher determined.

In his function of disciple-attendant, Munpa had visited the camps of the herdsmen of the region and obtained provisions, freely given to support the hermitage.

The guru was venerated because he was considered to be the spiritual descendant of a long line of adepts in doctrine and secret arts who all took the name of the glorious originator of the sect, Gyalwai Odzer (meaning victorious ray of light), and thereby proved, so it was believed, that they embodied the life and works of their predecessors.

A fantastic legend was told about the first Gyalwai Odzer. This legend, believed to be authentic, had no fixed origin in time because the nomads of the region, the Tibetan province Tsinghai, could not, not even vaguely, indicate a date. The legend, however, was clear enough, so well known that it was no longer discussed, for everybody had been told the tale during childhood. It had become a dogma, to be believed passively without even trying to ascertain its probability or validity.

Once, so the legend said, there had lived one of these fabulous masters who had succeeded in obtaining occult powers. His name was Gyalwai Odzer and he trafficked with gods and demons who either wanted to help or who were forced, by his manipulations, to be of service.

The *nāgas*, or watergods, were no exception and emerged

whenever the master approached their lakes or rivers to offer him treasures they guarded jealously in the crystal palaces hidden deep under the surface.

But the master, whose voracious spirit wanted to dominate all and everything, demanded more.

The day came that one of the princes of the liquid depths could no longer resist the master's magic and showed himself, bowing humbly, with cupped hands, holding an object. "Take it," the nâga said.

He offered a large turquoise, as blue as the sky, unbelievably luminous.

"Listen," the nâga said. "Have you heard of the jewel that grants all wishes? It has been given to the inhabitants of the divine worlds.

"Would owning such a jewel be a real asset? The sages doubt it. The gods who, in paradise, pick the fruits of virtuous deeds accomplished in previous lives only rarely obtain true knowledge. Real insight eludes the self-centered, for it provides a perfect view into the original nature of things. The gods are tainted by desire, and desire will project them into further incarnations, in the realms of the spirit and perhaps also into earthly life. They are propelled by blind impulses. Gratification of their senses leads to identification with objects. Whatever constitutes the objects will modify the spirit that embraces them.

"Apart from the jewel that provides desired objects," the nâga said, "our palaces contain many others, each imbued with a different virtue. The turquoise that I bring you is a fragment of the Very Excellent Jewel, of infinite value, for it provides penetrating insight which can measure the substance of all things and discovers the laws that direct them. With such knowledge your power will have no limits.

"Look at the turquoise brought to you from the watery empire. It is charged with occult energy. This is the first time it is exposed to earthly light. May it also be the last time.

"In the future, nobody should either see or touch it. Enclose it in a reliquary which, in turn, should be covered in cloth.

"When you leave for another world you will give it to your most worthy disciple who, without opening it, will pass it again to his most worthy disciple. That way, along with the spiritual lineage that will form itself before long, your successors will carry the marvelous talisman hidden under their monastic robes."

Having spoken, the nâga dived back into the azure waters of Koko Nor, the great lake, and Gyalwai Odzer took the turquoise back to his hermitage.

The hermit followed the nâga's advice and ordered a small silver reliquary to hold the jewel.

From then on the supernatural power of Gyalwai Odzer increased considerably. At his merest wish, large rocks flew through the air, mountains changed their form, rivers left their beds and cut new ones and even reversed their currents at his bidding.

Similar miracles were performed by his immediate successors, but the later teachers carrying his name seemed to show less interest in demonstrating their magic. The details of the legend lost their contours in a fog of uncertainty. All that happened so long ago.

Even so, the line of teachers stretched on, and as each one of them carried the supreme jewel the faithful nomads continued to believe, even though no one had ever seen the talisman that no longer manifested its existence in any tangible way.

Around the great blue lake of the nâgas matters remained much the same. The seasons succeeded each other, supplying the rain needed to make the grass grow, or withholding it. The herds prospered, or were almost killed off by disease. Children were born in the black tents, and people sickened at times; death carried the aged away and also some of the young because of wars with other tribes or fights among themselves.

Is it necessary to see the gods at work in order to believe in them? Faith is a gift. The people moving about the Chang Tang possess it in quantity.

*

Having climbed the stiff ascent, Munpa Des-song stood on the hilltop, in front of the door of the hermitage. It surprised him that the door was half open, but it could be that the master had gone outside, as he did sometimes to perform certain rites that he did not want to be witnessed. Munpa pushed the door and went in.

It was almost completely dark inside, but Munpa distinguished the large angular form leaning against the back of the boxlike structure in which the hermit meditated.

He has plunged himself into deep concentration, Munpa thought. He had often seen Odzer withdraw like that and knew that the exercise could last many hours and lead to a state in which his normal senses would no longer function. Trying to make as little noise as he could, Munpa prostrated himself, got up again to place his bag in a corner, and sat down in the lotus position, resting his upturned feet on his thighs. He then attempted to direct his thoughts toward the lofty heights where the spirit of his master would be soaring in utter freedom.

*

Outside all was silence. An inexpressible peace held the impassive earth, spread out over the vast solitude of the landscape, indifferent to the busyness of beings who are born

5

from it and who, after some vain activity, return to be dissolved into their source.

Far away a wolf howled. In the hermitage nothing moved.

The dawn came, the clear and pristine dawn of Tibet. It crept through the cracks of the door, made out of old wood, badly joined, touched the disciple's forehead, disrupting his contemplation, reached out through the narrow room, gliding along the uneven rock walls, and finally illuminated the straight form of the hermit.

Munpa looked at Odzer. He saw the robe, crumpled and spreading out of the enclosure of the hermit's cushions, and the teacher's undershirt and naked arms. He jumped up, alarmed by the disorder, and stood in front of the hermit.

Odzer's eyes were wide open, giving his face a ghastly expression, and a trickle of blood, already dried, stretched from his temple to his cheek and formed a brownish stain on the neckline of the garment. Munpa also saw the loose cord, frayed where it had been ripped.

Hardly able to comprehend the visual facts, Munpa stood fixed to the floor, with his eyes riveted on the hermit's face, then sank down and sat close to the seat. His venerated master had been murdered!

Munpa didn't move for a long while, his mind empty of all thoughts, dumb, close to annihilation. Then, gradually, he began to reason somewhat.

Gyalwai Odzer murdered! But how could that be? Didn't the hermit possess superhuman powers, wasn't he in control of demons, of gods even, of all beings, of all things? How could anyone have killed him?

Who was the murderer? Surely not one of the herdsmen of the region. Could it be that Moslem Chinese soldiers had been patrolling in the Chang Tang? But how had they been able to find the hermitage? Why would they have wanted to seek out this holy place? To steal? Odzer owned nothing, except some religious books, two copper lamps that he lit every night before the statue of his guardian god, and — the magic jewel.

Ah! The broken cord! It had held the reliquary.

Munpa forced himself to creep closer and extend a hand that felt under the bloody garment. He also made it move amongst the cushions and in the folds of the robe. Nothing. The reliquary wasn't there.

Theft would have motivated the killer. Perhaps the robbers, roaming from camp to camp, had heard the herdsmen talk about the precious turquoise and decided to seize it.

But how could *it*, the miraculous all-powerful instigator of miracles, condescend to being stolen? Why hadn't it destroyed the criminals and thereby protected its legal owner, direct descendant of the first Gyalwai Odzer, who had received it from a nâga?

All this would have to be a fantasy, the work of a demon. Or, perhaps the master wanted to try him by causing an illusion that would soon fade away. Gyalwai Odzer would come out of his meditations, there would be no blood on his cheek, the reliquary would once again rest on his chest, and the old hermit would smile ironically.

Munpa prostrated himself once more and got up. His master hadn't moved. He saw the dried blood again, the crumpled robe, the frayed cord silhouetted against the yellow shirt.

He still doubted, however, in spite of the evidence so obviously displayed. Mechanically he bowed and touched the feet of his teacher with his fingertips. His hand touched a hard object, which he grabbed hold of without thinking. He saw it when he straightened out again. It was a wooden tobacco container, of the type that many Tibetans carry in the main fold of their robes, the bulging pocket secured by their belts. It couldn't belong to Odzer, as the hermit had not used tobacco. Munpa opened the door and studied the little box in the light. He shouted with horror, recognizing the box that belonged to his fellow disciple Lobsang. He had often seen Lobsang use it and even made a joke about it once, for Lobsang had tried to engrave a flower on it that hadn't come out well.

Munpa's questions disappeared instantly. The motive of the crime was clear, and the murderer had left his signature. When Lobsang bent down to grab the reliquary the little container must have slipped out of his robe and fallen onto the cushions.

It was clear now what Munpa had to do: find the criminal disciple at once, obtain the reliquary, and convince the herdsmen that the villain had killed the hermit, so that a court of elders could judge and punish Lobsang.

Finding Lobsang wouldn't be difficult. Munpa knew his tribe's camp wouldn't be far away, since the herds had ample feed and there was no need to move. It wouldn't take long to reach the camp, but first he would have to perform his last duties to his master. How?

To burn the corpse he needed firewood. There are no trees in the Chang Tang, so he would need help from several men, who would have to travel some distance to cut wood and bring mules and yaks for transport. Before burning, the corpse would have to be cut up so that some of the flesh, and even the bones, beaten to powder, could be fed as an offering to the vultures, in some special and pure location. All these things would take time and could not be done by one man. But Lobsang had to be caught right away.

Munpa made a decision: the funeral rites could wait until his return. First he would catch Lobsang, then he would call on the lamas to help with the disposal of the corpse and to perform the proper rites.

Munpa returned to the corpse and arranged it according to the rules of tradition. He crossed the legs on the cushions in the meditation position. He straightened the chest and bound it to the rear of the seat with Odzer's own meditation cord, which the hermit used when he settled his body for long periods of intense concentration, winding it around his loins and legs. He applied some scarfs, left as presents by visitors, to secure the chin and support the arms. The corpse changed into a sinister puppet, seemingly alive. Munpa worked on as he had done before, when householders called him to prepare a dead relative. He had also chanted the sacred texts then, but that wouldn't be necessary now for Odzer needed no instruction on his journey to the Hereafter.

When the sad work was done, Munpa filled the altar lamps with melted butter and lit them. He took some *tsampa*, preroasted barley flour, a few cakes, and a handful of dried beans from the provisions he had brought the previous evening. He arranged the food on small saucers and left them as offerings on a low table that he pushed across to the meditation seat.

When he was done, Munpa filled his leather bag with most of the remaining foodstuffs, which would no longer be of use to his master. He also took the money that the herdsmen had given him to be offered to the hermit. He felt no guilt, for the silver might be useful while pursuing the murderer.

He prostrated himself for the last time, spending several minutes with his face to the floor, got up, bowed, and picked up the bag. Outside he closed the door carefully and secured it with a large rock. Then he went.

In the cave, the hermit-magician Gyalwai Odzer, last owner of the miraculous turquoise of the nâgas, stayed behind, erect on his seat, seemingly engaged in profound meditation. The lamps burned quietly.

The afternoon reached its end, the reddening sun dipped toward the horizon, painting the mountains with great splashes of purple and gold. In the brief enchantment of the short Tibetan dusk the executer, a tiny somber figure amongst the immensity of the wilderness, departed to arrest the criminal.

WHILE MUNPA DES-SONG believed the old hermit to be meditating and was worried about bothering him, Lobsang got away, galloping through the darkness. He had murdered his master and terror tore at his heart, a terror caused by superstition rather than guilt. The demons that served and protected Gyalwai Odzer would be out to pursue him.

Munpa, who had been ordained as a monk, belonged to the clergy, but Lobsang was a layman who had become a disciple in order to make a more interesting career for himself, which a *lung*, to be granted by Odzer, would help along nicely. Lung means rule, but the common people believe that a lung is no more than a short ceremony that entitles the beneficiary to understand some of the Buddhist scriptures, gaining insight that should be of both moral and material value. Without a lung, sutra chanting is mere chanting; with it, there is some magic. The teacher who grants the disciple his lung transfers some of his power, but not much, as there are other ceremonies, performed with students who have practiced long and arduously, that lead to a more intense transmission.

Lobsang had been accepted as a disciple, together with

a few other herdsmen, and, as he showed signs of intelligence, Odzer taught him some of the basic principles of Buddhist doctrine. He had been allowed to spend time close to the hermitage.

Of course Lobsang heard about the jewel carried by his teacher, but he knew already of its existence and believed in the legend surrounding the turquoise. Being close to the talisman was something else, however, and its reality grew as he returned to the hermitage again and again. He began to think about its beauty, and, true Tibetan that he was, also about its commercial value. All Tibetans are potential merchants and all merchants are tainted, a little anyway, by greed. Lobsang's avidity was not sufficiently developed to lead him to crime, neither theft nor murder, and wouldn't make him consider the risk of putting up with the gods and demons which, the legend said, Odzer could command, but a simple incident, a common occurrence within the boundaries of the Chang Tang, suddenly transformed the pleasant rustic that Lobsang had always been into a man possessed by evil forces.

One evening he met a girl herding sheep close to the camp where she lived, and the unexpected encounter kindled a flame of lust that overcame all his other feelings, especially when she gave in to his advances.

Lobsang returned to her and Pasangma received the unexpected lover that the malicious gods directed across her path. She was pleased, and so was Lobsang, but he was by no means satisfied; for the girl, although she wasn't yet fifteen, was married and he could only meet her by stealth.

Kalzang, the girl's elderly husband, was a wealthy nomad, owner of several herds, bad-tempered and violent. His wife, Tséringma, hadn't borne him a son, and he grumbled, holding her responsible, although the fault might be his own.

Tibetan custom authorizes and even urges the husband to marry a second wife should his first bear no children, and Kalzang announced that he would marry once more.

Tséringma was a jealous and commanding woman. She wanted to object, but her intelligence prevailed and she found a poor family willing to exchange their daughter, a timid little thing, for what they thought to be a considerable payment. Kalzang got his second wife, Tséringma her servant; they both abused the unfortunate girl. Pasangma worked, doing the heavy chores that Tséringma directed her to do. Kalzang smiled and didn't interfere. What was it to him? He didn't love or even like the girl, she was only there to provide him with a son. Tséringma was a better investment, for she increased his property through her shrewd bargaining. She sold his wool at a higher price than he could negotiate himself, and she knew how to haggle when he rented his pack animals to the caravans traveling through the highlands.

How could his first wife be compared to this weak little girl who was afraid of everything and met every situation with tears? During the days Pasangma belonged to Tséringma, to be treated as the older woman pleased.

Kalzang's need of her made the girl nauseated and Tséringma beat her at the slightest excuse. After a while the girl rebelled and threatened to go home, and was whipped by Tséringma while Kalzang laughed. Pasangma realized that her threat was empty. Her father had died and her mother lived with her three sons and their wives. Her family didn't want her back and would certainly not repay what Kalzang had laid out for her, even if they could, for they were still poor. There was no way out and she lost hope.

Lobsang, at their second meeting, proposed to take her away with him. She accepted at once. Her enthusiasm matched her lover's, but Lobsang still had to work out how he would transform his desire into deeds. Where would they go? Where to obtain money to buy provisions?

The money was the only real obstacle, the rest seemed easy enough.

He had friends among a tribe who had no sympathy for Kalzang and his retainers. Kalzang had sent his herds into the tribe's fields and his men had wounded some of the tribe's shepherds when they objected. If Lobsang fled through the tribe's territory, he would be protected and Kalzang would hesitate to follow. From there he could go further, either making for China or for Tibet proper, perhaps going as far as Lhasa.

But the money? How to get it?

Lobsang lived with his parents. He owned only his horse and its saddle, a well-sheathed sword of poor quality, two blankets, a sheepskin overcoat, a thick cotton robe, and a waistcoat for special occasions. He needed all his possessions, especially the horse, and even if he sold some of the rest it wouldn't bring in enough. What if he waited? Tried to get a job with the caravans perhaps? But could he afford to wait? And he might not earn enough to fill his saddlebags with sufficient food to be able to travel a long distance. He would find a way. Meanwhile he told Pasangma to be ready and to look out for him. He would come to fetch her, one evening, soon or a little later, he didn't know exactly when yet, but he would definitely come for her.

Pasangma was ready, every evening, on her return from the fields where Kalzang's sheep grazed.

*

The wilderness of the high northern mountains is dangerous for the man whose brain is feverish with passion, for he may begin to hallucinate. All around Lobsang, desperately thinking of a solution to his problem, voices whispered. It seemed that the wind murmured in his ears, sometimes insidious, sometimes caressing, always obstinate:

"Don't worry, there is a remedy, it's close, quite close."

"This jewel that Gyalwai Odzer owns . . . what good is it to him?"

"It has been so long since the turquoise left the palace of the nâgas, and it has been so long since the hermits used it to accomplish their miracles, by now its magic will have evaporated, but it still carries a high price."

"In China the powerful governors have grown very rich. What wouldn't they pay for such a giant turquoise?"

"And in China you will also meet with the great merchants who travel as far as India and Mongolia. They will offer good money, for they can resell the jewel easily and profitably."

"You have been told that Gyalwai Odzer goes into meditation every day, mornings and evenings, so deeply that the world is lost to him."

"He won't feel it when you remove the reliquary holding the jewel. All you have to do is cut the thin cord that is around his neck. You won't do him any harm."

"If Gyalwai Odzer is such a great magician as he is supposed to be, he will call a nâga and have the turquoise replaced. And if he can't do that, what do you have to fear? He won't dare admit that the talisman, the relic that has been left to him by his teacher who got it from *his* teacher, all the way down his famous line, has disappeared."

The wind sang on and pushed down the tall grass, each stalk becoming an individual in an audience, agreeing with what the wind suggested.

"Make up your mind, Lobsang. Pasangma longs for your arrival. Don't let her wait."

The mist rising from the marshes swirled into shapes. He saw himself receive money, buy merchandise, sell it again at profit. Bit by bit he would become rich. Then, some-where in China or Tibet, a powerful merchant — himself — lived an agreeable life among a wealth of bales of cotton and silk, carpets, furs, wool, and other goods that became more and more varied, and each night, going home, he would find Pasangma in his bed, the girl with the glowing skin, so soft to feel and possess.

The wind whispered on while the mist illustrated its temptations.

Lobsang made his decision.

*

Hidden near the hermitage, Pasangma's lover saw Munpa Des-song leave on one of his customary trips to beg provi-sions on behalf of his master. He knew Munpa would be away for three or four days and that he would have enough time to execute his plan and get away at leisure.

The idea of killing the hermit never occurred to him. The very possibility would have made him quake with fear. It would be merely a matter of removing an object without being discovered, an object that was, after all, of no use to its present owner. That same evening he should be able to succeed.

There was a delay, for three herdsmen arrived just after Munpa left the hermitage. They came to visit Odzer, perhaps for advice on personal matters.

Their tent was placed just off the path to the cave, and they were in no hurry. They cooked noodle soup in a large pot, sat around their fire, went off to spend hours with the sage, came back to drink tea and beer, stayed up late and rose early.

Lobsang was at their mercy, there was nothing he could do while the visitors dawdled. Munpa would be coming back soon. Odzer's timetable would be disturbed, Lobsang could no longer be sure at what hours the hermit would be meditating, oblivious to a stealthy hand reaching for the reliquary. Perhaps, what with the herdsmen disturbing him, the hermit would not be able to meditate at all.

Time passed slowly and Lobsang's impatience increased. Finally, during the afternoon of the third day, the herdsmen left. Lobsang could not afford to wait longer — it would have to be that same evening.

*

The sun sank behind the mountains as the traitorous disciple touched the cave's door. He sneaked inside and prostrated himself to test the hermit's concentration. Should Odzer talk to him or acknowledge his greeting in any way he could either leave or stay if the master told him to do so. Besides, he still respected his teacher, out of habit perhaps, and feared him. He would rob Odzer certainly, but nevertheless . . . Conflicting thoughts battled in his mind while he got up and looked about. It was dark in the cave, but he could make out the hermit's sitting body by the light of a small lamp on the altar. Odzer's tall shape, dressed in a dark red robe, didn't move. Lobsang shuffled forward and touched the small table in front of Odzer's seat that held a box of tsampa and a large bronze teakettle.

Odzer's half-open eyes seemed to see nothing. He was surely meditating — his mind would be thousands of miles away. Lobsang bowed and stared. No, the eyelids never moved. He might as well be invisible, he *was* invisible.

Lobsang moved forward a little, placing himself between the seat and the table. He would have preferred to stay like that, to restrain his trembling hand, but he fought his fear and reached out, felt the hard metal of the reliquary, touched the thin cord that supported it, and heard himself shout.

Gyalwai Odzer's eyes were wide open, enlarged inordinately, fixing the cringing robber, appearing like glowing cinders emitting arrows of fire.

Lobsang's hand groped about for something to use for protection. It grabbed the teakettle and raised it. The heavy bronze hit Odzer's temple: the fierce light in the hermit's eyes died away.

The murderer no longer thought. His movements became mechanical, he did what he had set out to do. The cord broke, leaving the reliquary in his hands. He hid it under his own robe and rushed away without looking back. He ran to the place where his horse waited, saddled it, and galloped down the path. By then it was dark.

Munpa wouldn't return until the next morning. Lobsang, whipping his horse, was still riding then, and the cold wind hurting his face sobered him to the point where he could think again. No one would ever know that it was he who had killed the master. He was sure he had left no clue. But was the hermit really dead? Perhaps the kettle had only stunned him, in which case he would name the criminal, the thief of his treasure. And wasn't Odzer a magician? The stunned hermit would have ways and means to discover Lobsang. He would take revenge.

And even if he was dead, a dead magician could be more dangerous than a live one. The cave would only hold his corpse; Odzer's spirit was about, right here maybe, at the head of an army of demons. Any moment now he would see those large eyes again, fiercely red, charged with power.

Lobsang's stupor changed into a wave of madness. He dismounted when the dawn crept across the landscape and hid his horse amongst tall weeds near the side of a brook. He stayed there all day, sleeping fitfully while his horse moved about, grazing in the weeds.

When he woke, the terror had subsided somewhat and

he was able to plan ahead. He had seen no one since he left the hermitage and nobody would have seen him while he slept, for a herdsman meeting another will stop to chat and find out where the other came from and where he is going. Everything seemed all right so far, but he still had to find Pasangma, without being noticed on the way.

He took time to prepare his tsampa with water from the stream, ate, and saddled his horse. When darkness once again covered the highlands, he set out.

His reprieve didn't last. During the night the phantoms were with him again, appearing in odd corners, always following, laughing maliciously. He spurred his horse, but the demons kept up easily, even passed him, and made threatening gestures. Insanity grabbed the murderer's brain.

He reached his goal before the morning broke, a place well away from any path. He wasn't far from his mistress now. She would be herding her sheep in the next valley. He would seek her out in the evening and meanwhile rest. He was sure she would be in the appointed place, wanting nothing but to be removed from the cruel couple who made her life a misery. And besides, she loved him. He knew he wanted her too, the lovely girl for whom he had just committed a terrible crime.

What if she couldn't come that night? She might be ill. Perhaps a servant would be sent in her place. If so, there would be nothing he could do. If he showed himself there would be questions, questions he could never answer.

But there was no point in worrying. He had to stay and wait, then rush off with Pasangma the minute he set eyes on her. When the sheep didn't return to Kalzang's camp herdsmen would be sent to investigate.

All day he waited and worried in spite of his effort not to. He preferred to fantasize about his immediate problem for his turning thoughts kept the demons away. He couldn't sleep and sat staring at rocks and weeds. Toward evening the girl showed up, smiling with pleasure, and gave him the bit of food she had managed to steal from the camp: a little tsampa, a piece of dried cheese, and a few ounces of butter. If Tséringma had caught her she would have been beaten, but her thoughts of Lobsang and the great adventure had given her courage. Lobsang thanked her gratefully. His horse was ready. He lifted the frail girl into the saddle, mounted, and kicked his horse with his heels. There was no time for a tender embrace, a pleasant word. Each minute counted, and soon the camp was well behind them and the immensity of the Chang Tang Highlands stretched ahead.

The horse, well rested and of exceptional strength, carried the couple with ease. No one seemed to follow, and after several hours Lobsang thought they might stop for a moment.

"Eat quickly. We'll be riding until dawn."

The girl didn't reply. She was happy, in her own way, like a small passive animal that knows it's been taken care of.

"We won't have a fire, as it's too dark to find dry weeds and the flames will betray us. If Kalzang's men see the ashes they'll know in which direction to pursue us. By tomorrow they'll be hunting for you."

"Yes," Pasangma whispered, "but not here, Lobsang. Kalzang will believe that I have returned to my family. Some weeks ago, when Tséringma beat me again, I said I wanted to go home. Kalzang was there when I spoke. They'll remember my words."

The information reassured Lobsang. Pasangma's mother and brothers lived to the north of Kalzang's camp, and they were traveling south.

*

Pasangma was right. When that evening Tséringma didn't see her sheep come back she thought at first that Pasangma had been looking for edible roots again and forgotten the time. When the darkness increased she sent a servant to fetch the girl and the animals. He didn't find her and even when he climbed a hill there was no one in sight. The sheep had separated and were wandering about unhappily. He couldn't leave them, the wolves were never far away. He shouted as loudly as he could. No answer. So he collected the sheep and drove them home.

Kalzang didn't think of a possible lover, but it was clear to him that Pasangma hadn't been happy in his tent and that the girl was frightened of Tséringma. She was his property, however, and he meant to retrieve her and punish her so that she'd never run away again. His fists itched, but he would have to wait until the following day. There was no point in chasing her during the night, when she could evade him easily. She had surely gone back to her family, and he would find her at her mother's camp the next day.

But Pasangma wasn't with her relatives, who swore that they hadn't seen the girl since her marriage. Kalzang asked them to repay him. Hadn't he given them two yaks and some silver? With the girl gone he was suffering a loss. They refused and reminded him that they weren't obliged to reimburse him. They would pay, certainly, but only if Kalzang could prove that the girl was somewhere. Where had she gone? And if she was dead, where was the corpse? Perhaps he had sent her away, or even killed her. If that was the case, her family wouldn't have to recompense the loss. Kalzang knew the law, but he refused to withdraw his claim. He thought of Tséringma and the way she would revile him if he came back emptyhanded. He grudged her her victory. Tséringma would be delighted that his second marriage had ended in disaster. But he could still strengthen his case by recouping his investment.

Both parties insisted and a jury was formed and asked to judge the case. The jury members arrived rubbing their hands, for it's customary to feed and lodge them in style, and they were so looking forward to daily helpings of plenty of beer, some gin, and large chunks of roasted meat that they weren't in any hurry to reach a decision. Pasangma's brothers grumbled since they had to provide the meat, and Kalzang's temper matched theirs as he paid for the liquor. But he wouldn't give in, and the jury listened patiently and kept on adjourning, because there would always be another day.

Pasangma didn't return, and the men sent out to look for her took their time. They preferred not to battle the Chang Tang and found comfortable places to camp, where they sat around their fires, talking and drinking.

While the jury pondered, Kalzang found a soothsayer, who had to be paid before consulting his books of spells. He threw dice, added their results, and made calculations. Finally he nodded and told Kalzang that the girl was already far away, that her feet weren't touching ground, that it was all very mysterious but that he knew a way of luring her back. His method involved asking some friendly gods for help, but gods demand offerings to be purchased for money. Kalzang made an effort to smile and paid the required fee. He never saw Pasangma again.

*

Naturally Lobsang knew nothing about these events. He believed Pasangma and assumed that Kalzang was wasting his time in the north. But he didn't believe her altogether. Perhaps Kalzang was cleverer than the girl thought. He hurried on, although he stopped to eat and rest. And the girl was so beautiful he couldn't resist wanting to make love to her, and she didn't object when he did.

"We won't stop here very long. It will be dangerous if we delay." But he stayed longer than he had intended.

He satisfied his desires, but his mind wasn't at rest and

when they rode off again he wouldn't talk. His fear had returned. There wasn't enough distance between him and Kalzang, and certainly not enough between him and the hermitage. He tried not to think of Gyalwai Odzer but to concentrate on practical matters. He rode on, in spite of the danger, for it was day now. He had been lucky so far. They hadn't met anybody, perhaps because the grasslands were changing into a desert, unattractive to the herds and their attendants. Still, it would be better to hide until dark, and he found a tiny hill, hollowed out into a cave, where they spent the rest of the day.

His goal now was the Chinese border, where there would be some little towns in which he could sell the jewel. After pondering this possibility, he discarded it. The border was too close, and he might be recognized by Tibetans from the highlands who went there to sell skins and wool. Even if his countrymen wouldn't know him personally, there would still be questions: What tribe do you belong to? What brings you to China? He couldn't afford the risk; any fool could see that he was a herdsman from the Chang Tang. The death of Gyalwai Odzer would soon be known, even at the border, for the tribes move about and individuals travel far. Everybody talks to everybody.

He began to forget about Kalzang and his men, for the vision of his teacher staring at him became too strong. How could he show the jewel to some small merchant in China where it might cause talk that would travel back home? China was vast, however; he might get there via some other route. As long as he could get out of the Chang Tang where any encounter might be dangerous indeed! Perhaps he could stay in Tibet and travel as far as Kangting in Sinkiang where, he had heard, many merchants gather.

They left the cave as soon as darkness allowed, and he walked next to the horse so it wouldn't tire with the weight of two people. They progressed slowly, but they were now in the desert, where only the very few travel. Certainly at night there was little chance of meeting anyone. Pasangma was enjoying herself. She felt free, and the new situation, with her lover so close, seemed marvelously pleasant. No longer a slave, and riding under the stars. Whereto? She didn't care. Did Lobsang have enough provisions in his saddlebags? The question hardly touched her brain. She felt like a wild bird; nothing could harm her. She was flying away.

Lobsang couldn't share her delight. He made her dismount and enjoyed their mutual passion briefly, but his fears came back immediately afterward.

There was still enough to eat, for several more days perhaps, and soon they would reach a town where the turquoise could be sold.

A town? Which one? Kangting seemed a bad choice. The merchants would be suspicious. But where else could he go?

Lobsang knew his native highlands but very little about what was beyond them. He had listened to those who had been outside his own province of Tsinghai, but what seemed fairly clear then was vague indeed now. Still, he had to go as far as he could, create physical distance between himself and the corpse of Odzer erect on his meditation cushions. He could see every detail of the tall angular body as well as the grinning demons that danced around him.

He would have to get rid of the jewel attracting them and change it for silver, which would be of less interest to his pursuers but of immediate use to himself.

He hadn't dared open the reliquary so far — he had heard that it was made in the shape of a lotus flower. Here, in the empty desert, he couldn't risk the confrontation. Later, in a marketplace, with people around him, the power of the nâgas might be less.

But he had to wait, even if the jewel tortured him more

and more. It burned into his chest. Sharp claws protruded from the reliquary and tore at his skin. The pain became so intense that he began to mumble. A little later he yelled and Pasangma looked at him. She was frightened too now, and her fear increased as she saw him change for the worse.

They wandered on for several more days, haphazardly, silently, for Lobsang, unable to explain his suffering to the girl, refused to speak. Even she knew by now that they weren't going to China in spite of what Lobsang had told her at the beginning of the journey. They weren't going to Kangting either. Where was he taking her? Did he know himself?

One evening she took courage and asked. Lobsang threw his tea bowl down and jumped up. "We go to Nepal."

Nepal, the country of wool, she had heard of it. People went there as pilgrims to venerate the holy buildings commemorating events relating to the life of Buddha and his disciples. Where could this country be? She believed it was somewhere in the southwest. Very far away.

Lobsang hardly knew what he was saying. He had thought of the country on the spur of the moment. Why shouldn't they go there? The further the better. He had forgotten Kalzang completely. The man could come, take his horse and Pasangma, beat him up for all he cared. He was fleeing from Gyalwai Odzer, but the image of his teacher, alive and all-powerful, was as close as if he were still with him in the cave in the cleft of the hill. Would he ever be able to escape this terror? *It*, whatever it was, was after him, so close that it could hurt him at will, and the ever-present demons carried the shapeless fury. He could hear them laugh and whisper to each other. They spied on all his movements, knew his thoughts, amused themselves by speaking to him, so articulately that he could hear the words the wind wafted into his ears.

To silence them he made love to the girl again, rudely

and with all the energy he could muster, but the words went on. They were laughing again, hundreds of demons, and others echoed the piercing joy of their fellow fiends. Their shrieking multiplied until it filled the desert, and reverberated against the faraway mountains, coming back at double strength. Lobsang pulled free, pushed the girl away, and ran, collapsing in the rough sand, holding his ears to block out his shrieking tormentors. But the furor went on, even when he hid his head in his robe and his body rocked to and fro helplessly.

The couple moved on. The days passed. The stages of their journey became shorter and shorter. Often Lobsang stopped at midday and lay in the sand, motionless but unable to sleep or even rest.

Pasangma no longer asked where they were going. They had rationed themselves from the start, but now there was little left in the saddlebags and she called on the houses that had begun to appear, ordered by Lobsang to sell her bracelets for food. The silver bracelets, Kalzang's only gift, were all she had. She didn't want to give them up, but they had to eat in order to be able to reach the place where, Lobsang said, they would become rich. Which place? Nepal? How far could that fabulous country be? Of the three bracelets only one was left. She told Lobsang, but he didn't answer. At the next village he sent her to trade it. She went alone, while Lobsang hid himself and the horse. The villagers might want to take the horse and its well-made saddle. He couldn't trade the saddle either, for they would enquire about the horse and might swarm out to look for it, knowing he was too weak to protest. Lobsang knew the ways of his country. He had practiced them himself, he and his brothers. Pasangma, ugly now because of her privations, could pass as a pilgrim, as she carried nothing but a bag made out of cheap cloth. There are so many like her wandering about the country, she wouldn't arouse suspicion.

The moment came when there was nothing left to eat. Pasangma suggested, in a hardly audible whisper, that he might sell the reliquary. She had never seen it, but she knew it was there for it had hurt her often during their lovemaking. Most Tibetans carry, while they travel, a little reliquary that contains the image of a god or a protective charm. If Lobsang's was made of silver they might sell it for a considerable sum of money, or trade it for an ample quantity of food, enough perhaps to last until the end of their journey.

But Lobsang, when he understood what she wanted him to do, yelled at her, and she didn't have the courage to repeat her request.

Although she didn't regret being liberated from the tyranny of her husband and Tséringma's sadism, she had begun to think that she hadn't really gained much by following Lobsang, whose moods alternated between extreme depression and sudden fury. She no longer loved him and doubted whether she ever had. He had been a means of escape, no more. As matters stood now she might have to escape again. It occurred to her that she could ask the people of the next village to take her in. She clenched her hands into trembling fists. No! They would ask her where she came from. Kalzang's arm was long; it could reach beyond the desert. She also had to consider what Lobsang would do. The man was mad now. She looked at him as he stumbled next to the horse, muttering and gesticulating. If only he would calm down. Nepal might be close. Perhaps a foreign country and the proximity of many people would calm his mind. Once again she could only resign herself to her fate. Meanwhile there was no food, they had been fasting for three days, her strength was ebbing. They had seen camps in the distance, but Lobsang kept going, for there was nothing left to sell except the horse and he needed the horse.

They could still find feed for the animal because it was spring and the sparse brooks were banked in by vegetation.

27

The horse, well rested because of their many stops, was in good spirits. Lobsang, eyeing it from time to time, thought of leaving Pasangma and racing off on it — if he were alone it could easily carry him to safety. He had difficulty remembering that he had stolen the turquoise and killed the hermit for the girl. All his desire for her had gone. She was a nuisance, a burden slowing him down. Her passive presence irritated him, and he hated his companion now and could leave her without regret. He shook his head, trying to be rid of the pain. The horse might be in good condition, but he wasn't. Nepal was still far, he might starve, have to eat the horse, and still be on the wrong side of the border. He clenched his teeth and tried to order his weakening spirit to keep going. Out there nobody could trace him, and he could tell as many lies as he pleased. He vaguely remembered that the cities of Nepal were some distance from the border. Where was the border anyway?

He could reason only when the terror abated, but now he was tortured by hunger. There was only the horse, and he wouldn't sell it. "I won't, I won't," he mumbled. The jewel? The way he looked now he would be taken for a thief; he would be arrested, questioned, beaten if he so much as mentioned the turquoise.

Pasangma, stretched out on the sand, cried miserably.

Another night came, bringing more suffering, and the next day promised no relief. The reliquary seemed the only way out. He hadn't taken it from its cover yet: it would be of silver, surely, with some gold filigree here and there. A valuable piece, but the poor herdsmen living in the black tents they now passed once in a while wouldn't be able to pay a proper price. Even so, selling it wouldn't get him into more trouble. Pilgrims often sell their religious possessions when they run out of provisions. If he offered an empty reliquary for sale, the buyer would immediately assume that he was keeping its contents, a talisman, a miniature Buddha cast in bronze, the portrait or small statue of some teacher.

He would remove the jewel and keep it until later, and the reliquary would provide the wherewithal to reach the safety of Nepal, buy him impressive clothes, give him a chance to recuperate. There was no choice. This time he would approach a camp by himself. He couldn't trust Pasangma with an article of value. She might run away with it, or sell it for a handful of copper coins. He would wear his sheepskin coat, wash himself in the next brook, ride to the camp, tell them that his companions were waiting for him so that the herdsmen wouldn't be tempted to knock him down and steal the reliquary. The possibility of leaving Pasangma in the desert presented itself again, but he chased the thought away, telling himself that he could consider that part of his problem later.

Now that he had reached a decision he felt a bit better, but he still preferred to wait until darkness before unwrapping the reliquary. He would rather commit the sacrilege in a safer place, with the protection of a town around him, but the darkness would have to do instead. If it was dark enough he wouldn't be able to see himself reach for the jewel.

His thoughts had proceeded to that point when he heard howling in the distance. He shivered. A bad sign. Wolves? Of course. He recognized the long-drawn-out trembling notes. Once again he saw the dead hermit, sitting in his meditation box, his back supported by the boards forming the enclosure of the seat. He pushed the image away with all his remaining strength. Wolves — they might be chasing his horse soon. He called the animal and tethered one of its front legs to a convenient rock.

It was getting dark. He lit a small fire and told Pasangma to watch it, while he picked more dry weeds. "There are wolves about."

29

"Did you hear wolves?" asked Pasangma. "I heard nothing."

Lobsang didn't answer. So he alone heard the wolves. Were the demons hunting him again? He crept close to the fire. His heart fluttered, and he could feel his stomach move. His very bones seemed to rattle about in the empty sack that his body had become.

This was the moment.

He felt under his robe and pulled out the reliquary.

"You're going to sell it!" Pasangma shouted, mad with joy. She would be eating soon and they could continue the journey that would lead to the happy life Lobsang had talked about so long ago.

Lobsang stared at her with such undisguised hatred that the girl threw herself on the ground, hiding her face in her hands.

Lobsang pulled out his knife and cut the cloth covering the reliquary, which had become even dirtier and frayed at the seams. The reliquary appeared, dull with age. It was indeed made of silver, of superb craftsmanship, decorated with golden ornaments, each holding a minute pearl. It was far more beautiful than Lobsang had imagined, eminently worthy to protect a supernatural jewel.

He held it in his hand for a while and finally persuaded himself to open it.

It was stuffed with more cloth, of a pale blue color. He tried to unfold the cloth. It had been cut into a strip and he unwound it slowly and carefully. His fingers felt for the hardness inside as the strip became longer. He stretched it between his hands, undid the last fold. Nothing. The reliquary had been empty. And he, in order to secure this non-existent miraculous turquoise, had killed his master and surrendered his mind to hosts of evil foes.

With a leap he was on his legs, throwing the reliquary on the ground and giving vent to an inhuman shriek.

Frightened by the horrible sound, the horse jumped, broke its rope, and raced off into the night.

Lobsang froze for a moment, paralyzed by fear and anger, then ran after the fleeing horse.

Pasangma didn't move.

Lobsang had never told her that the reliquary contained some precious object. She didn't know of his crime and couldn't understand the insane fury that possessed her lover. All she could imagine was that the horse had run away and Lobsang, who had seemed to hear the howling of wolves, had gone to retrieve it.

Finding a horse at night isn't easy. Pasangma couldn't help Lobsang now, she could only wait. She picked up the reliquary and began to polish it with her sleeve, cleaning it of the earth that sullied the silver. When she was done she let it slide into her bag.

The night proceeded slowly, silently; its serenity surrounded the girl. Lobsang didn't return. From time to time she fed the fire with dry weeds, so that Lobsang would be able to find her again. Her anxiety grew. It might have been that the horse had strayed into a herd of wild donkeys and that they had persuaded it to join them to live the free life. If that happened they would never see it again.

Dawn colored the horizon. Lobsang still hadn't come back. The growing light showed nothing but empty desert and, far away, the dark line of mountains.

Born and raised among the herdsmen, the young woman had often seen horses escape. Usually it took several days to capture them again for they would stray far. If Lobsang had found the horse he would be back by now. She got up and set out, after having arranged the saddlebags and killed the fire.

She had walked awhile when the sun came up, lighting up dark shapes that whirled about in the sky, planing easily.

Vultures, Pasangma thought, and her heart lost a beat.

Hadn't Lobsang heard wolves during the night? They could have killed the horse and the vultures would be feeding on the remains of the carcass. But nothing was certain yet; there could be some other dead animal ahead.

She hurried on, pushed by fear. The vultures were circling close by now. When she reached the spot that was the center of the birds' vigil, she saw the skeleton of the horse, picked clean already, and a little distance from the bones she found Lobsang's corpse.

It had lost most of the facial skin and its robe was torn, bloody flesh hanging from the tears.

Dumb, unable at first to comprehend what she saw, Pasangma stood stuck to the earth. A little later she was running, straight ahead until, at a safe distance from the sinister spectacle, she swayed and fainted.

MUNPA DES-SONG had been given his name
when he was ordained as a monk, and reached
the rank of *trapa*, in the small monastery
where his father took his last and superfluous
son. The name means "he who passed through
the darkness" and is an appropriate reminder for one who,
supposedly, longs for nothing but the divine light. But now,
while striding through the highlands, he longed for nothing
but the apprehension of the murderous Lobsang and had no
time to look at the large hermit rats (so called because they
sit so still that they appear to be meditating) who were sunning themselves until, disturbed by the determined Munpa,
they returned grumpily to their holes. In the distance a herd
of wild donkeys spied on his movements, large ears stuck up,
but continued to graze once they were sure he wasn't coming
their way.

Munpa marched on, on his way to Lobsang's camp. He
was tired from having traveled the long distances necessary
to collect provisions on behalf of his teacher, but also because
of the emotional strain of the previous night. He forced himself to keep walking. He never stopped to rest or have a
meal, and when evening came and his strength gave out, he
dropped down and rested where he fell. His thoughts re-

mained centered on the jewel, and unruly, half-defined ideas surged up and joined each other in sudden fantasies. The turquoise, passed by master to disciple, symbolized the teacher's final transmission of power. The Tibetans believe that the vital principle of an individual may reside in an inanimate object, an animal, or a plant or tree. It may be said "this rock, this tree, this bird is the 'life' of that lama, that chief, Mr. So-and-so," and it is understood that any damage or harm inflicted to the symbol will hurt the person it represents. The turquoise, Munpa thought, might be the "life" of Gyalwai Odzer, but the last Odzer hadn't been able to transmit his power for it had been taken from him.

Munpa endeavored to think more clearly. Couldn't it be that the theft of the turquoise had caused his master's death? But the turquoise hadn't been destroyed, and it would certainly refuse to lend its power to a criminal who obtained it by force. So, if he, Munpa, would retrieve the reliquary, and return it to the hermitage . . . and, yes, attach it once again to the cord around Odzer's neck, wouldn't his teacher then return to life? And bless his servant by touching his shaven skull with both hands?

The intensity of his thoughts made him hallucinate. He *saw* the figure of Gyalwai Odzer, illuminated by a great light against the background of the night. Waves of devotion lifted Munpa and made him float into a whirlpool of ever-increasing bliss until he imagined that his very spirit came apart in the ultimate blessing of complete annihilation. Overcome by emotion, he stretched out on the ground and fell asleep.

The next day he arrived at the camp of Lobsang's relatives. Disappointment waited for him: Lobsang had left some ten days before. He hadn't told his brothers where he was going, but they assumed that he would have found temporary employment with a Chinese caravan bound for Hsi-ning, a transport of wool that had been short of men. Lobsang had said nothing about visiting the hermit. Munpa listened politely. He knew that Lobsang had never joined the caravan, but the word Hsi-ning stuck in his mind. Hsi-ning is a Chinese town of some importance, and Lobsang would want to sell the jewel. There would be rich merchants in Hsi-ning. The more Munpa thought the clearer it seemed that Lobsang could have gone to that city. Very well, he would follow him there.

Hsi-ning, to a simple herdsman, is a metropolis of enormous proportions. Munpa had visited Hsi-ning before, and now again he felt lost in its crowded streets, and gaped at the impossible variety of articles displayed in the stores. He studied the good things to eat, the fine clothes, and the utensils made out of metal and porcelain. Often he didn't know what purpose these articles could have and he would wander away, shaking his head. There was no point in asking. They were so expensive that he didn't even consider the possibility of possessing them.

He also observed the fat storekeepers and tried to calculate their wealth. Would they be rich enough to buy the giant turquoise, as blue and radiant as the holy lake of the nâgas? Munpa didn't think so. But there would be other merchants, elevated above the storekeepers. Perhaps these nabobs were in contact with governors and princes, even the emperor himself, the semideity in Peking, dwelling in a palace similar to the spectacular abodes of the gods. Munpa had an idea what these places looked like, as they were painted on the walls of the little monastery where he had received his early training. Now where could he meet these all-powerful merchants?

He timidly inquired. The storekeepers weren't helpful at first, but he finally found one who could speak Tibetan and was directed to an enclosed shopping center specializing in luxuries. Munpa visited the mall but wasn't impressed; the trinkets displayed weren't too valuable.

He began to worry. It seemed that some of the merchants were a little suspicious of the ignorant foreigner in his tattered robe. Could it be that they suspected that he, Munpa, had perpetrated a crime himself and might be looking for a receiver of stolen goods? Why would a poor monk wish to meet an important merchant? What sort of articles would a monk sell?

About a month had gone by since he had left the hermitage. Would anyone have followed him? It could well be that the master's death was still a secret; sometimes nobody visited the hermitage for months on end. But Munpa, the disciple-attendant, was supposed to show up regularly at the neighboring camps and villages, for he had to beg for provisions and silver, pass messages, and run errands. His absence would surely be noted. One of his fellow disciples might have taken it upon himself to visit the cave to make sure that everything was all right. What would the disciple think if he found Odzer's body tied to the meditation seat? Would he connect the murder with Munpa's truancy? And hadn't Munpa disappeared *after* he had been seen returning to the hermitage, loaded with food and money? Wouldn't the suppliers of these articles be tempted to jump to conclusions? Where was the silver, the tsampa, the butter? What had happened to all these gifts to the hermit?

He knew that he had taken Odzer's property with the best intentions. He wasn't accusing himself, but the others might think differently. And meanwhile time had passed: he had traveled to China. The herdsmen were bound to misinterpret the attendant's motives and attempt to catch him. If they did the outcome would be clear. Nomads don't care for subtle details and far-fetched explanations. Their actions are prompt and definite.

His summary left him no choice. He couldn't return to the Chang Tang without Lobsang's bound body in tow. And he also had to find the turquoise, or proof that the murderer had sold the jewel. But would the nâgas' treasure allow itself to be sold? Munpa's faith in miracles didn't allow him to believe in the possibility, even if the turquoise had permitted its holy owner's violent death. The apparent contradiction was too great a problem for the simple trapa's mind, and he finally overcame it by adding yet another miracle, to be accepted without questioning. *Gyalwai Odzer was not dead.* The hermit only pretended to be dead, for reasons unknown to his disciple. As soon as the turquoise was returned to the cave, the master would resurrect himself, even more powerful than before, for the knowledge gathered during his sojourn in the plane of the spirit would be added to his wisdom.

Returning to more realistic considerations, Munpa reminded himself that he belonged to the clergy and that the monastery of Kum Bum was close by, within walking distance. The monastery, although situated in China, was of Tibetan origin, and the monks were his countrymen, willing to advise him if properly approached. It wouldn't do, of course, to disclose the exact nature of his business, but perhaps he could invent some clever story. He set out at once.

Luck was with him when he arrived. The guards at the gate knew a wealthy trapa who sometimes rented rooms to guests, and they directed him to the monk's house.

Munpa, although amazed at the size of the monastery, recognized many details of its daily routine. The vast temple complex was run along the same lines as his own monastery in the Chang Tang. Tibetan monks know no vows of obedience and poverty, and pay their own expenses. They may be kept by relatives, be wealthy in their own right, be working for wages, or trade. Some live in luxurious mansions, others in miserable huts, but everyone has his own home, where he

37

eats, sleeps, studies, and meditates. Only a few rules apply. All resident monks are expected to join the communal morning and evening meditations in the large assembly hall, and nobody can leave the compound without permission from his superiors. Only the *tulkus*, who have gained their insight in previous incarnations, and the lamas, who have completed their training in their present lives, can move about as they please.

Munpa presented himself as a pilgrim, eager to venerate the birthplace of the great teacher Tsong Khapa and to bow to the miraculous tree, marking the site where this saint incarnated, the tree that shows religious images on its leaves. He also told the trapa that he was investigating a rather unpleasant matter — something to do with an unscrupulous colleague from Tsinghai who had promised to do a poor widow a favor. He said he would sell the woman's necklace of amber and agates in Hsi-ning. The money was to be spent on a statue of the Buddha and some religious books that the woman wished to place on her altar. The man left for China and was never heard of again.

The trapa nodded sadly, and Munpa prided himself on the vagueness of his story. It was just what could have happened, what *had* happened, to an old lady of his acquaintance some years back. While his gullible audience commiserated Munpa opened his bag and presented the monk with some butter. The trapa accepted the gift and told his guest that he wouldn't have to pay rent.

"If you don't mind sleeping in a corner of my warehouse."

"I won't mind at all, sir," Munpa said happily.

It turned out that he wouldn't have to pay for his meals either. That same day, on his way back from the holy tree, he met with another monk who had just bought several horses and was looking for somebody who could take care of the animals. Munpa offered his services and was taken to the man's stable, where they agreed that he could eat lunch and dinner at the horse trader's house and that he would feed the animals, rub them down regularly, and walk them a few times a day. Munpa accepted gladly. Walking the horses would give him an opportunity to meet all sorts of people who might provide him with information.

Little by little, Munpa settled back into a well-known and comfortable way of life. Kum Bum might be an architectural wonderland housing more than three thousand monks, but its atmosphere didn't differ in essence from that of the humble cluster of buildings where he had lived before and that also belonged to the sect of the *gelugspas*. The *gelugspas*, or Yellow Hats, split hundreds of years ago from the Red Hats, the original Buddhist order of Tibet, which, according to the Yellow Hats, became lax in its ways and needed stringent reforms. Munpa's admission into Kum Bum permitted him to join the morning and evening meditations and be served some meals in the great central temple, but he preferred to be free to roam about at will. Tea was usually available in the kitchens, and he fixed his own breakfast and held up his bowl twice a day at the horse dealer's house, where it was filled with ample helpings of hot, rich noodle soup. Meanwhile he took care of the man's animals and found time to wander about the halls and other public places.

His deeper mind remained concentrated on his quest, and each evening the hermitage appeared to him and he bowed to the west. He also had visions of the great blue lake of the nâgas, providers of the turquoise. The visions weren't too clear. The truth was that the well-fed Munpa was having a good time, safely tucked away in a warm spot, with congenial work and plenty of friends who spoke his language. Even so, the desire that brought him to Kum Bum would not allow itself to be ignored. He continued his investigation and ran into a monk who had some knowledge of the jewel trade. They sat down and talked at length, and somehow turquoises crept into the conversation. All Tibetans are fond of turquoises, including the clergy, and most religious statuary is adorned with the brilliant blue stones. He was told that the larger jewels are often bought and sold in Lan-chou, a city to the south of Hsi-ning. Munpa returned to his lodgings, pondering the matter again. Hsi-ning was still close to Tibet, Lan-chou much further away. There were a lot of Tibetans in Hsi-ning and hardly any, according to the monk, in Lan-chou. Lobsang might have considered Hsi-ning an unsafe market for stolen property and headed straight for Lan-chou. The new theory seemed even more probable when Munpa considered Lan-chou's proximity to the capitals of China's more prosperous provinces. He was told that Lan-chou is also close to Mongolia. Mongolian princes keep splendid courts, and they often buy their jewels in China.

"I will go to Lan-chou."

"Beware," the monk said. "You haven't met the true Chinese merchant yet. He is sly and cruel, and he'll never admit to being a receiver."

"I'll be careful." He announced his departure to the horse dealer.

"I'll be sorry to see you go. Why don't you wait a few days? I've sold some horses to a firm in Lan-chou. You can go with my servant, who is taking them there. It's better to ride than to walk, and I'll take care of your traveling expenses."

Munpa couldn't refuse, although he was irritated by the further delay. What would Lobsang be doing now? Would the thief have stayed in Lan-chou or have traveled on again? And what proof did Munpa have that he was on the right track? Munpa wouldn't admit to his confusion and preferred to rely on his faith in the miraculous turquoise and its power to revive his master in the hermitage. So far he might not have come up with a single intelligent plan, but his quest was just. He convinced himself that he was being helped along by supernatural forces and experienced, several times during the following days, an intoxicating mystical ecstasy. These blissful moments were, in turn, proof that he was on the right path.

*

Hsi-ning surprised and impressed Munpa; Lan-chou devastated him completely. The nomad, raised in the remote highlands where all is quiet and any meeting is a memorable event, wasn't prepared for the turmoil of a real city, and he wandered about in a haze, bumped by the jostling crowd. The luxurious stores, the stately houses, the palaces, their walls painted with intricate murals, resplendent under upswept roofs supporting golden dragons, the flowering gardens, the temples with their elaborate statuary of gods riding on clouds, the fragrance of incense everywhere — the naive rustic gazed and gaped. Lan-chou, wonder of wonders!

But he wasn't altogether lost. On the recommendation of his acquaintance, the horse dealer's servant, Munpa found lodging in a caravansary. The inn was busy. Several caravans, bringing exotic goods from Mongolia and Turkestan, had arrived simultaneously. The innkeeper, a Mr. Chao, was prepared to employ Munpa. He had to help stack the merchants' goods and take care of their animals. Once again he was provided with free room and board. Munpa accepted the job, but grumbled secretly. Surely he hadn't left his homeland to become a stableboy in China. But he worked hard so that he could take a little time off every now and then to visit Lan-chou's stores and markets. His zeal would be rewarded, but not quite in the way he expected.

The unfortunate herdsman, ill at ease in this alien environment, entered store after store, enquiring about jewels, stammering his story about a necklace of agates and amber. The shopkeepers mistook him for a customer, showed their wares, and lost patience when they realized their error. Gradually Munpa began to see the foolishness of his approach. He was after the great turquoise and should stop wasting his own and the merchants' time. But could he go back to the stores he had already visited? Just then he saw another jeweler's sign. This time he tried to tell the merchant the truth but got tangled in his explanations. He gestured and stuttered, trying to think of the correct words in Chinese, and didn't notice that the manager was whispering to an assistant and pointing at the door. Soon two constables came in, accused Munpa of wanting to steal, and grabbed him by the arms.

The well-built Munpa resisted. Although he was brought up as a monk, he knew how to fight. Munpa's swinging fists made contact and the slender constables staggered and fell. He ran for the door but found it barred by the storekeeper. The assistants had run outside and were yelling for help. A crowd gathered, and more constables arrived. Munpa lost the ensuing free-for-all. He was beaten, kicked, and dragged to jail, where he proclaimed his innocence to a bored sergeant. The sergeant referred the case to the magistrate.

"When will he see me?"

"Who knows? Take him away, men!"

Badly battered, totally exhausted, Munpa found himself in a dank room, part of a motley ragged crowd that examined the newcomer without sympathy, asking questions to which he could find no replies. He had been taken for a thief! What would happen to him?

Nothing happened. He sat down, leaned against a wall, and eventually fell asleep.

When he woke it was day again but the small holes serving as windows allowed little light to come in. Munpa discerned the other prisoners, sitting about or wandering in groups. Some hunted lice in the folds of their garments, meticulously killing the insects or setting them aside on the floor. The prisoners also squashed the eggs of their minute tormentors. The spectacle didn't interest Munpa. Tibetans also kill lice when they have nothing else to do. He felt hungry. Wouldn't the jailers bring him something to eat? Alas! No. The Chinese do not feed their prisoners. He remembered that Tibetan jails do not provide meals either. But he had expected better treatment in the sumptuous city of Lan-chou and felt cruelly disappointed. Still, there was no reason to lose courage altogether. The constables hadn't bothered to search him, so his small stock of silver was untouched. Money will solve most problems. Munpa sighed and considered his situation. To show his lumps of silver would certainly invite disaster. The other prisoners might gang up on him or try to rob him while he slept, with a knife at his throat in case he woke up before they were done. It might be better to wait and see. Nobody seemed to be starving, so how did they get their food?

He could hear people moving about in the courtyard outside and see bowls of rice and soup being passed through the unbarred windows. The luckier prisoners began to eat; the others watched them miserably. Some begged, others threatened. He saw some prisoners share their food with friends but felt too shy and proud to ask for favors.

The morning passed on. There were no more visitors, and the holes in the wall displayed nothing but empty sky. Munpa looked out and saw the heavily armed guards, an unnecessary precaution, he thought, for the windows were too small to squeeze through and most of the prisoners were hampered by chains and heavy iron balls.

His fast continued.

Then the vendors arrived, shouting to advertise their wares. Money clinked, large copper pennies were counted out, again steaming bowls passed through the windows. "How much for a sausage?" the richer prisoners shouted. "What price for a bowl of soup?" Munpa didn't know what to do. He had no coins, and it might be dangerous to ask the vendors to change his silver.

"Haven't you eaten?" a voice next to him asked.

"No."

"Don't you have friends or relatives who can bring you something?"

"No."

Munpa didn't think it would be a good idea to appeal to his employer, Mr. Chao, at his caravansary. It didn't matter to him that the innkeeper, an upright and pleasant man he had learned to respect, would find out that his stableboy was in prison, but Munpa was too proud to publicize his losing fight with the Chinese constables. The Chinese may think little of the savages who live beyond their borders, but their contempt is easily matched by the arrogance of the Tibetan herdsmen, who are convinced that the Chinese are a weak-kneed race of thieves who move by stealth and will always avoid an honest match of strength. Tibetans pride themselves on their status as heroic bandits, fierce warriors who will take on superior numbers of enemies and destroy them with their accurate bullets or fiercely flashing swords. The despicable dwarfs who sneak about in the dark are insects to them, to be squashed between their fingernails. Munpa might be at a disadvantage in China, but he was sure that a Chinese in similar circumstances would never have dared go to Tibet.

"Not eaten . . . no friends," the voice at his elbow continued. "But soon the *hochan* will be here. Maybe tomorrow. He always brings bread, rice, and other things to eat. See him as soon as he arrives. He is a monk who belongs to a monastery whose chief is very powerful. The magistrate listens to what that chief says and if the hochan wants you to be released you will be free soon. Ask to talk to his superior."

A hochan is a Chinese monk. Munpa nodded and thanked the prisoner. There was some hope again. He could tell the hochan that he, Munpa, was a monk too. Satisfied, he did what he always did when no particular activity was demanded: he stretched out on the floor and fell asleep. His dreams carried him back to the peace of the Chang Tang and made him forget his present predicament.

*

The hochan, a monk belonging to the Buddhist Zen sect, lived in a moñastery that influenced much of what went on in Lan-chou and was permitted to enter the jail whenever he pleased. Toward the middle of the morning, one of the guards opened the door and bade the monk welcome. Munpa, wide awake now and torn apart by hunger, was waiting eagerly, but when he saw the hochan he forgot all about food and felt helpless with mirth. The hochan, flanked by his acolytes, two boys who carried baskets loaded with food, looked exactly like a comical character from the religious theatrics of Tibet.

The figure represents a major part in a philosophical controversy that occurred in Lhasa during the reign of Teson dé Tseng, the Tibetan ruler born in the seventh century. A Chinese teacher arrived at the court and expounded the doctrine of *wou wei*, involving a method to reach supreme enlightenment through doing nothing. Kamasila, an Indian teacher also present at the court, defended the accepted method of Tantric Buddhism, which believes in magic spells,

45

chanting sutras and mantras, the use of mandalas, and elaborate exercises that will, eventually, lead to transmission of insight and power. When the chronicles of the period are studied, it seems clear that the doctrine exposed by the Chinese was far superior to Kamasila's teaching, but the Tibetan ruler was not impressed and the jury he set up declared that the Chinese sage had lost the argument. The sage, accompanied by his two assistants, returned to China.

In the following centuries the misunderstood philosopher was ridiculed in Tibetan plays. During the important religious festivities, the sage returns and the actor who takes the part dons a yellow robe and a large mask that exaggerates the Chinese features. The constant expression on the mask contrasts with the actor's body gestures and creates a comical effect of supreme stupidity, mimicked by boy actors who gambol about their superior. The Tibetan audience howls with pleasure when these clowns arrive, and each year the number is the highlight of the religious fair. Munpa had seen and enjoyed the act many times and was reminded of it now. He couldn't help himself, he had to laugh. When the hochan and his acolytes turned toward him, Munpa saw that they were indeed the exact images of the actors in his favorite show. Soon he was doubled up with mirth, hiccupping and slapping his thighs.

The well-trained hochan didn't lose his composure, but the acolytes fidgeted, wanting to laugh too.

Munpa, aware that he was creating a scene, made a supreme effort and managed to calm himself. With acute presence of mind, he explained to the hochan that the sudden sight of so much food had caused an attack of insanity and that he hadn't eaten in two days.

Was the monk moved by compassion? His expression didn't change, but he inclined his shaven head, filled a bowl with soup, and gave it to Munpa.

"Don't you have anyone to care for you here?"

"I don't know anyone in Lan-chou."

"You are a nomad from beyond the border."

"I am a Tibetan," replied Munpa. "A lama." He knew that the title implies that he who is so addressed has finished his studies and is qualified to teach. But the Chinese call all Tibetan monks "lama." This wasn't the moment to correct their error.

A flicker of comprehension moved across the hochan's face.

"What was the magistrate's verdict? How long do you have to stay in jail?"

"He hasn't seen me yet," replied Munpa. Seeing that the monk had done with him and was ready to pay attention to the other prisoners, he added a request. "I have a little piece of silver and would like to change it for coppers so that I can buy some food tomorrow."

"Give," the hochan said quickly.

Munpa felt about in the pocket of his robe and dropped a small piece of silver into the acolyte's cupped hand. "It's all I have," he muttered sadly.

"I'll send change tomorrow." The hochan moved away, followed by the acolytes, who were imitating his solemn gait and mannerisms.

"You see, my advice was good," said the prisoner who had talked to Munpa before. "Did the hochan say that he would mention your case to his chief?"

"No."

"Never mind. He will anyway. His monastery is called Temple of Transcending Wisdom of Supreme Serenity, and you'll find it on the other side of the river. As soon as ·they let you out of here you should go there. They'll take care of you because you're also some sort of hochan in your own country. I heard you say so."

"It's true," Munpa affirmed.

"That's some more good advice I have given you."

Munpa understood and shared his bread. The prisoner grabbed his piece and rushed off to a corner to eat it in peace.

The next morning one of the guards called for Munpa. "This money is yours. The hochan sent it."

Munpa was sure that the fellow had already helped himself but returned some coins to the hand that was pushed into his face.

Several days passed. The hochan came again and moved about the jail without paying attention to Munpa. The acolytes ladled soup into his bowl and distributed bread.

Munpa was buying food from the vendors now and had enough to eat, but he was nervous about the other prisoners. He had seen some of the stronger ones looking at him. He tried to sleep as little and as lightly as possible. His small stock of coppers began to diminish, and he worried about the length of his stay in the disgusting dungeon.

In desperation he concentrated on the power of his teacher. Hadn't he left the Chang Tang to continue to serve Gyalwai Odzer? Hadn't he passed from failure to failure because of devotion to the hermit? But his effort dissipated into thin air. He couldn't even evoke his master's image. He was too tired and too miserable to collect his thoughts.

At last, three weeks after Munpa's arrest, the hochan told him that the second secretary of his monastery had spoken to the magistrate. "You will leave here the day after tomorrow."

But even this move wasn't destined for completion. The next day a turnkey announced that all the inmates of the dungeon were to appear before the magistrate at once. Guards chained the prisoners together and marched them to the courthouse. A clerk read the charges; constables made their reports. The judge listened without interest and dispensed assorted punishments: so many months in jail for this one, so many strokes for that one. The kneeling prisoners shuffled forward when their turns came.

Munpa faced the magistrate and tried to stammer a protest. He hadn't broken any laws, he had merely made an enquiry at a store. The judge lifted a limp hand. "Ten strokes."

"And then?"

"Then you can go."

The guards were in a hurry too. They dragged Munpa outside, stripped the robe off his back, and pushed him onto the ground. Two constables took turns hitting him. A third counted. The skin on Munpa's back tore away under the cruel bamboo. "Ten." The constables kicked him, and he managed to scramble to his feet. He was pushed through the door of the court. "Away with you."

He found himself in a street. He was free.

THE SEVERE beating that had almost crippled him left Munpa's spirit untouched, for the time being anyway. He arranged his robe and looked about him in the street. He felt for his purse; it was still there. His back stopped hurting for a moment. All was well, more or less. He stumbled into the sunlight, found a restaurant at the next corner, and sat down on the first empty chair.

He ordered tea, the Chinese tea that, compared to the rich Tibetan brew, tasted like nothing, for it hadn't boiled properly, was drawn from just a few leaves, and didn't contain butter, salt, or soda. Only its warmth provided some consolation. His stomach clamored loudly, its cramps more urgent than the pain in his bleeding back and hips. First things first: he ordered an ample meal of *momos,* steamed meatballs, properly spiced, and a large helping of chicken soup, stiffened with mushrooms and noodles. He thought while he ate.

Demons, undoubtedly, interfered with his plans. Who but the denizens of the lower hells would dare to waylay his efforts to serve his holy master, to revenge Odzer's unfortunate fate, to restore him to the living? Perhaps there had been some demons that Odzer hadn't had time to subdue. If Munpa returned the turquoise, the hermit would certainly take care of these devils. It had to be so — Munpa, slumped on the hard bench, nodded sadly to himself, continuing the fantasy that was growing into a full-length novel — with a proper beginning, an acceptable plot, and a happy ending. But he was still in the middle of his fabrication; there were still the demons to take care of. He would eat first and plan later. He needed rest, quiet, and, why not, a drink. The waiter brought him a cup of Chinese gin. Munpa sipped it and ordered another.

"An inn?" he asked. "Close by?"

"Just around the corner, sir, to the left when you leave."

Munpa tipped the waiter gratefully. In his present state he wouldn't be able to walk far. He left the restaurant, doing his utmost to walk straight so that nobody would notice his condition. He stopped at a store and asked for butter, thinking that he might rub it into his wounds to alleviate the pain, but there wasn't any. The Chinese don't use butter, as they abhor its rancid smell.

He found the inn. It wasn't first-class but met the conditions by which the Chinese define comfort. Built out of dried clay, without an upper story, it enclosed a large yard, consisting of rooms on three sides and stables on the fourth. Each room had one or two *khangs*, beds on top of the tiled stove. Munpa hired a smaller room, paying extra for the privilege of having it to himself. As he carried no baggage he had to pay in advance.

His robe of crude cotton, soaked in blood, stuck to his wounds, aggravating his pains. Not having any butter he considered sending for a doctor who might apply a soothing balm but discarded the thought. The doctor would immediately understand what had happened to him, and he didn't want to be known as an ex-convict. The shame of his predicament! Munpa refused to submit to shame; he preferred

51

to suffer, for his master, for a just cause. He remembered the story about the great Tibetan saint Milarepa. Milarepa, a disciple of the harsh guru Marpa, had been ordered to build a house on a hilltop. Marpa wouldn't instruct Milarepa until the house was built. Milarepa complied, carrying enormous stones up steep slopes, finally finishing the dwelling. Marpa said there had been some mistake, it wasn't the right hilltop. Would Milarepa be good enough to wreck the house and rebuild it on that other hill, over there? This procedure was repeated several times. Milarepa kept on carrying rocks up steep slopes and dragging them down again. The unfortunate disciple's back was covered with running sores, but Marpa showed no pity. In the end the ordeal was over. Marpa, not needing another house, never went near Milarepa's structure but finally condescended to teach his student.

Munpa knew the story by heart. He remembered a passage and chanted it to himself: *"With sores on his back, and blood and pus running down."*

In spite of his pain, Munpa sniggered. Milarepa had been *ordered* to build the houses, but nobody was ordering Munpa around. He had thought of his quest himself. Every effort so far could be traced to that original voluntary decision, when he left the hermitage in the Chang Tang such a long time ago now. He hadn't been promised any special initiation, hadn't been urged to comply with any particular condition. That his merit might be favorably compared to Milarepa's improved his mood and anesthetized the violent stinging of his sores. He stuck his head out of the door and shouted for a drink. While the liquor seeped through his veins, he lay down on the khang and mumbled, with devout ardor, fragments of Milarepa's hymns to his teacher Marpa:

"I prostrate myself at the feet of my Buddha-like master . . . I give you my body, my word and my mind . . . I beg you to stay alive for as long as all beings have not reached the Knowledge that liberates from rebirth and death."

The contents of these songs had never been very clear to Munpa. They weren't clear now. But he enjoyed his recitation.

*

The next day Munpa got up late, considerably sobered, both physically and mentally. His pains, no longer dulled by alcohol and mystical fervor, were even worse than the night before, and his dirty robe, rubbing against his back, had inflamed his wounds. The sturdy Tibetans' pain level is usually quite high, but their endurance is nevertheless limited. He managed to struggle off the khang but could hardly move about in his room. He didn't think that his condition would improve. The pains might even get worse and he couldn't stay in the inn forever. To return to the caravansary was out of the question. Besides, he was supposed to work in the stables. How could he work if he couldn't even stand up? And how would he explain his sojourn in jail and the humiliating sentence the uncaring judge had imposed?

He would have to go somewhere, somewhere close. Whom did he know except his employer at the caravansary? Munpa sighed. Of course, the hochan. The hochan was only a lowly monk, but hadn't he mentioned Munpa's case to such a lofty personage as the second secretary of the monastery called Supreme Serenity? This powerful priest might not have been able to prevent the beating — perhaps the message wasn't passed to the magistrate — but it had effected his present liberty. Yes, he would go and see this secretary to beg a favor. Munpa was a monk after all, a Buddhist monk. The Zen priests were Buddhists too. Buddha is compassionate. The favor would be granted. He didn't want much: a quiet room, some food, medical treatment. He would leave as soon as he could — but where? Munpa groaned. Later, later. The quest would have to take care of itself for a while. There might be some hint . . . a miracle perhaps.

53

He managed to leave the inn and stagger into the street. A rickshaw appeared. He hoisted himself into it painfully and asked the coolie to take him to the Zen monastery on the other side of the Yellow River.

How would he announce himself? He knew very well that a secretary, even if he was of the second rank, would not easily see anyone who appeared out of nowhere. The coolie had been running for a good while and they hadn't reached the river yet. But when Munpa finally arrived he still hadn't thought of a suitable approach.

The monk at the gate didn't help. He stood and stared, waiting for Munpa to say something. A minute passed. "Well," Munpa said at last, "you see, I was in jail and the hochan . . ." He stuttered through his explanation and ended by mentioning the second secretary. "Do you think he would see me?"

"Wait here," the monk said.

"You see, I want to thank him and perhaps —"

"Wait here," the monk repeated, and shuffled into the temple.

Munpa waited unhappily, unsure of what he would do if the secretary didn't remember what the hochan had said about the prisoner who claimed he was a Tibetan monk. But the priest evidently did remember and the gatekeeper returned and took Munpa to the secretary's office.

"Where is your monastery? Are you a Red Hat or a Yellow Hat?"

"I was ordained at Dayway-ling in the province of Tsinghai, but I left my monastery to become attendant of the guru Gyalwai Odzer."

"Where does this guru live?"

"Also in Tsinghai, in the Chang Tang, in a cave. He is a great saint. He spends most of his time in meditation."

The secretary showed some interest. "Really? And what method of meditation does your teacher use?"

54

"I am his attendant," Munpa replied humbly. "My master has other disciples whom he instructs. I only take care of the hermitage. I'm not capable of understanding his high doctrine, but I've heard the disciples say that he teaches them the meditation of *the great emptiness* and of *nonactivity.*"

All Buddhist priests are familiar with these terms, and the secretary of the Supreme Serenity became even more interested.

"And how did you get into jail?"

Munpa hesitated. He wasn't sure how far he could trust the secretary.

"I was in a store," he replied. "The merchant wanted to throw me out. His assistants pushed me, I pushed them, constables arrived . . . I also pushed the constables."

"Pushed? You mean you fought with them. But why would the merchant want to get rid of you? What were you doing?"

Munpa felt he was losing ground. The questions became too pointed. Would he drag out the old story of the necklace of amber and agates? It hadn't been a good story to start with. What sort of connection would a monk have with a widow? The Chinese priest's quiet eyes never left Munpa's face. The priest was obviously very intelligent. Would he tell him about the turquoise?

The priest waited. Munpa plucked at the sleeve of his robe. "I am following a thief. The thief might have offered the object to a storekeeper. I visited the storekeepers."

"What object?"

"A Tibetan reliquary."

"Was it yours?"

"No, not mine."

The secretary understood that the Tibetan visitor did not want to divulge more information. The man carried some secret. Perhaps he should be allowed to keep it.

55

"Good. So finally you were released from the prison. Did the magistrate see you?"

"He did, but I don't know if he was the one you spoke to. He didn't ask me any questions, didn't even want to listen to my explanation, and . . ."

Munpa was in pain. He could feel the pus from his sores trickling down his back. Would they send him away? He needed treatment, a little ointment rubbed into the wounds.

"He had me beaten," Munpa murmured, blushing with shame and rage.

"He had you beaten," the secretary repeated. His face didn't express any particular feeling. "How many strokes did they give you?"

Munpa's blush deepened. "Ten."

"The skin broke?"

"Yes. There's blood on my back," Munpa whispered.

"Very well," the secretary said calmly. "You belong to the clergy, so you can stay here."

An acolyte fetched Munpa from the secretary's office and led him to a cell where he served him tea. A doctor appeared a few hours later and studied the wounds without asking questions. He applied a salve to the sores and told the acolyte to bring a clean cotton robe. "I will come back tomorrow." He left without a greeting.

Munpa had succeeded. His requests were granted; for the moment he didn't wish for anything else. Yes, food perhaps. He was hungry again. Didn't these Zen monks eat? He hadn't breakfasted at the inn, and it was almost evening. He waited another hour before peeping into the corridor. There was nobody in sight. He slipped out of the cell.

"Where are you going?" the gatekeeper asked.

"I'm hungry," Munpa stammered. "Haven't eaten all day. Do you know if there is a restaurant in the neighborhood?"

"You don't have to go out to eat. Meals will be served in your room at the appropriate times. Go back. The doctor ordered that you should rest."

Munpa didn't want to rest, but he could only thank the gatekeeper and return to his room. He sat down sadly. The hard khang wasn't too comfortable either.

At sunset a young monk brought him a tray. Munpa studied the small bowl of rice, a piece of salted cabbage about a foot long, some dry bread, and a pot of tea. The monk left the tray on the khang and left quietly.

Munpa muttered in Tibetan. "Is this the evening meal? No wonder these fellows are so thin and pale." He ate, taking his time. The rice was almost cold, but the salt accentuated the taste of the cabbage somewhat. He was longing for a chunk of fried meat and a handful of butter. His stomach rumbled; the small helpings had lost themselves in one of its corners.

*

The cell darkened, and he looked out the small window. He saw an empty court and heard sharp hollow sounds. Somebody was hitting a thick board with a wooden hammer. The rhythm quickened and Munpa smiled. The sounds were familiar. He was reminded of his small monastery in the Chang Tang. There a copper bell was hit, also with a wooden hammer, and, in the same way, before the evening meditation started. Seven slow beats, then one, and two quick ones, then again, quicker and quicker, then five. All over again. Then three. One more. Two short beats, one final long one, ebbing away, floating, diminishing, dying. The copper sounds were more melodious, but this instrument, whatever it was, had its charm. Munpa could not be called a poet, but his soul was touched and he stretched out on the khang, his mind partly filled with undefinable but pleasant fantasies that changed into a vague dream, deepening into sleep.

The next morning the same monk woke him and gave him some bread and a large bowl of the weak tea that Munpa didn't like.

This meal was a special favor. The Zen monks didn't eat until midday. The second meal was identical to what he had been served the night before: rice, cabbage, bread, and more tea. The doctor came in the afternoon and checked Munpa's back. Munpa wasn't wearing the clean robe so the doctor made him change and called for the acolyte, who took Munpa's filthy garment. "It will be washed. The dirt is bad for your wounds."

Munpa nodded, trying to hide his surprise. Wash his robe? Tibetans *never* wash their clothes. Their robes last until they fall apart. Dirt is part of the trapa's life. There is no soap in Tibet. But there might be some wisdom in what the doctor said. Now that his wounds were cleaned they felt better. He knew that they would heal by themselves, but there could be no harm in expediting the process. He would leave as soon as he recovered, the quicker his recovery the better. The jewel was still out there — the turquoise, the life of his teacher.

The doctor called every afternoon for several days. His ointment and detached concern, combined with Munpa's sturdy life force, improved the patient's condition. Scar tissue was covering the wounds and his fever had gone down. Munpa would have felt fine if he weren't hungry all the time. He attempted to ignore his stomach and forced his mind back to the jewel.

Discarding logical planning, which had brought him nothing but trouble, he dreamed of a miracle. He still had some faith: the supernatural forces would take pity and help him out. But nothing could be expected to happen in the simple quietude of the Zen monastery. He would have to leave, expose himself, make himself visible to the gods. He promised himself to seek out the secretary again and obtain his permission to depart.

It may be stated that Munpa never had a chance to make his own plans. That evening, after dinner, a monk came into his cell. "Tomorrow our abbot will see you," the monk said. Then he left.

The abbot would be an enlightened guru. Munpa told himself that any meeting with a guru is a blessing. But he wasn't looking forward to the interview. The teacher would be asking questions.

*

When he was taken into the superior's room, Munpa greeted the master in Tibetan fashion. He prostrated himself and raised his cupped hands, symbolizing his willingness to lift the dust off Buddha's feet. Then he came to a kneeling position, folded his hands, and bowed. The superior inclined his head briefly. "Seat yourself."

Munpa crossed his legs, tucked them under his robe, and straightened his back.

He had never met a Chinese guru before. The simplicity of the room struck him as peculiar. The high lamas of Tibet live in palatial surroundings and are seated on thrones amongst age-old statues of Buddhas, teachers, and gods. Little light is allowed to filter into their rooms and there are tapestries and *tankas* — elaborate scrolls — depicting demons circled by flames, glaring horribly. Butter lamps flicker, a gong is struck, incense smoke curls up slowly. The visitor is awed by mysterious splendor, impressed by the proximity of forces that he cannot understand. He mumbles his request and the guru advises him, quoting from scripture. The lama blesses him by touching him with silk cords suspended from an ornamental stick. On rare occasions the teacher lowers his hands and allows them to rest on the visitor's head.

But there was no mystery about this small, well-lit room. The abbot sat in a comfortable chair next to a small table. The walls were painted white and adorned with brush drawings. Munpa was faced by a meticulous simplicity and a complete absence of trappings.

The teacher's face, although old, didn't show a single wrinkle and was devoid of expression. Munpa could discern no sympathy, but no hostility either, no contempt, no interest. He was looking at a wall without cracks, hiding the secrets of the guru efficiently. The Tibetan felt as if some heavy weight were pressing on his mind. What questions would the master ask? And what explanations would Munpa offer in reply?

The abbot spoke at last. "You have a teacher in your country. You said that he teaches the doctrines of *great emptiness* and *nonactivity*. Speak to me about this teaching."

Munpa had expected anything but that particular question. He didn't know what to say. The abbot waited without showing any sign of impatience.

"I . . . I . . . I'm only the simple attendant of my guru," Munpa stammered. "He hasn't deemed me worthy yet of explaining the truth. I told your secretary that I overheard conversations between my master and other disciples."

The abbot didn't reply. His unmoving eyes seemed to change their expression. Munpa told himself that this guru was "looking within" just as Gyalwai Odzer used to look within when he absorbed himself in his meditations.

"You will return to your teacher?"

Munpa couldn't lie to this living statue. "My master is dead."

But he had hardly finished his sentence when he began to tremble. What had he said? Was it the truth? Surely Gyalwai Odzer wasn't dead. No, absolutely not. The hermit was only waiting for the jewel to come back to the hermitage. Hadn't he seen him, as a vision, that first night when he was on his way to Lobsang's camp? To say that his guru was dead was committing a sacrilege. "He isn't dead . . . I don't know . . . he lives . . . He lives in another way . . . I don't know . . ."

The abbot remained as calm as before. Time passed in silence, a silence that hurt Munpa to the core of his being. He was used to the silences of Gyalwai Odzer, but this Chinese applied silence as a weapon. Munpa would prefer questions. He couldn't bear the eyes looking within and the quiet thin mouth of the abbot that seemed chiseled into his face.

Every resistance became impossible. Without being aware of what he was saying, Munpa began to talk. Gradually he told the abbot everything, his return to the hermitage, the night with the corpse, the terrible surprise when morning came to the cave, Lobsang's tobacco container, his own immediate pursuit of the criminal. He related the events of his subsequent journey and its miserable end when he was beaten in the jail's courtyard. He talked mechanically, like a man who is hypnotized, but the memory of his unjust punishment woke him from his stupor.

He looked up and realized that the abbot hadn't asked him to relate what had brought him to the monastery. Perhaps he should explain what he meant by his teacher still being alive "in another way."

The abbot seemed completely detached from what was happening in his room. Munpa felt like a bird glued to a branch, flapping its wings in panic. He wanted to scream with frustration. He prostrated himself again. The words pushed each other to escape from his mouth. He told the abbot about the miraculous turquoise presented by a nâga, about Gyalwai Odzer's glorious predecessor, about the jewel being handed down from teacher to disciple, again and again into the present, until now, when it was robbed by an ingrate, a criminal. He had sworn to catch Lobsang and wouldn't rest until the jewel could be returned to the torn cord dangling around Odzer's neck. He related his vision of his teacher and the resulting knowledge that Odzer was still here, or "there," "in another way." He had felt his guru's hands on his head. The turquoise . . .

All strength left Munpa's body, and he lay at the feet of the abbot, utterly exhausted.

"Get up and return to your room," the abbot said softly.

"What do you want me to do?"

"Nothing. Look at the wall."

The abbot raised his right hand a fraction of an inch. The gesture made Munpa's body tremble. He knew he was dismissed, and scrambled to his feet, bowed, and left the room.

In his cell an acolyte, again an exact replica of the comical character in the Tibetan religious play, served him tea and a piece of bread. But this time Munpa didn't laugh. He drank the tea, sat on his khang, and faced the wall.

That night he slept deeply; there was no room for dreams. The meeting with the abbot seemed to have destroyed his mind.

It was still shattered when he woke the next morning. The day, interrupted by the monk bringing his meals, passed without registering while he sat and stared, indifferent to what might be going on.

*

The doctor announced that further visits would be unnecessary. The wounds on Munpa's back were almost healed, and he was given some ointment so that he could finish the treatment himself.

Munpa remembered the abbot's advice, and, accepting it as an order, began to "look at the wall."

62

Three days passed while he stared. Munpa knew, although he had never been asked to submit to this discipline himself, that similar methods were used in Tibet. Tibetan gurus instruct their students to concentrate on some object, on the naked surface of a large rock, for instance, or on a sky uncluttered by clouds. He had heard that unexpected results are obtained in this way. Gods may suddenly show themselves to the contemplating disciple; all sorts of helpful visions may occur. But he doubted whether observing a wall would lead to any spectacular results. He noted that the walls of his cell were covered with frescoes showing a large number of different scenes, episodes apparently taken from everyday life, although some depicted unusual images of supernatural beings. All personages were in miniature and the backdrops were of equally Lilliputian proportions, so that the walls were literally crawling with a diversity of happenings, creating the impression of an intense existence.

As soon as he stopped viewing the murals as pretty illustrations, he became aware of a wealth of detail. The artist had gone to great lengths to make his figures realistic, and it was easy to see what their gestures, expressions, and general bearing were meant to express.

After several days of solitary contemplation, Munpa began to amuse himself by explaining the attitudes, behavior, and exploits of the little people surrounding him. As he became more interested, he chose heroes from the helmeted warriors, merchants, monks, lovely princesses, fairies, and demons. He also invented stories for the characters. That traveler over there, attacked by horsemen, was an exiled prince searching for a new kingdom. The people staying in a miserable shanty were being visited by some important lady; they were a statesman and his family, in temporary disgrace, but still secretly favored by some members of the court. The monk carrying a bundle of clothes, striding along brandishing his staff, was going to India to be instructed in some of the more subtle aspects of Buddhism. Gradually all figures studied by Munpa were invested with some purpose and he began to predict the outcome of their adventures. The knight crossing the drawbridge of a castle, probably on his way to transmit an important message, would be made welcome and thanked. But *then* what would happen?

Munpa lost interest in the knight. There was that other young man, asleep among tall weeds. A fairy was floating down from the clouds to wake him. Who could this young man be? An ardent student, surprised by fatigue? Or a lazy fellow who preferred dreams to study? There was a book, face-down in the grass. What did the fairy want of him? Was she going to take him with her into the sky? Munpa imagined one complete short story after another, playing a part in each one as he identified with the heroes. He had never fantasized like this before, but the ardor of his quest could have interfered with his customary rustic stupor, or the scanty meals of the temple of Supreme Serenity may have caused some chemical change in his brain.

He didn't feel bored as the hours passed. Then, one day, he discovered a scene he hadn't noticed before. Between some large rocks a hermit sat engaged in meditation. Munpa gasped. The memory of Gyalwai Odzer surged into his mind and he felt accused. What was he doing here, wasting his time imagining this and that and forgetting his promise? Wasn't Lobsang still free? And the turquoise still missing?

He jumped away from the wall and nearly bumped into the monk who brought him his lunch. He forgot everything when he noticed a dish of beans. No cabbage today. Kidney beans with a vinegar sauce. Amazing. It got dark after dinner, and he had no lamp. He slept peacefully that night.

The next morning he studied the wall but could find no trace of the hermit between his rocks. Perhaps he wasn't looking at the right spot. He followed the wall slowly, tracing the miniatures with his finger. Not here, not there. All day he searched, concentrating on each part of the wall. When the light faded, he still hadn't found the hermit.

He tried again the next day, finally concluding that he must have been hallucinating. To imagine that Gyalwai Odzer had sent him a sign was only a little step. He had been called by the hermit. Munpa wasn't sure what to do next. He could ask to see the abbot and beg for advice.

While he thought, he began to study the wall once more and discovered a trapa. The Tibetan monk, dressed in a russet robe, was a member of a caravan; merchants on horseback were followed by their heavily loaded camels and mules. He had looked at the caravan before and was positive that the trapa hadn't been in the picture then.

Besides, the monk was moving and had turned to face his observer. No doubt about it, this trapa represented Munpa himself, not just his portrait but his living image. Munpa felt himself walking along, part of the caravan of breathing and snorting animals. Another hallucination! He had left the khang, somehow penetrated the surface of the wall, and joined this procession of men and beasts. He cried out with terror, jumped away, wanted to flee. But some irresistible force pressed him to the wall. The trapa was still there but not as clearly as before, and in a different spot, moving deeper into the landscape.

Magic, Munpa thought, black magic. He tried to overcome his fear and made an attempt at reasoning. The abbot had to be a wicked sorcerer. No doubt all the people on the wall moved under his spells. They certainly weren't the handiwork of some decorative artist. Each and every one of them depicted a soul enslaved by the impassive magician who ruled this monastery. The abbot had projected them onto this wall and manipulated every detail of their lives.

Munpa ran from his room and shouted at the gate-keeper. "I want to leave the monastery immediately!"

"I will pass your message to the second secretary," the monk said placidly. "Wait here."

The gatekeeper was back within a few moments.

"The second secretary," he declared, "has ordered that you will take your own robe, which has been washed, together with the Chinese robe you have been given, and you must also take this." He handed over the robe and a small bag. When Munpa checked the contents of the bag, he found a pot of ointment, some biscuits, and a small piece of silver.

"Thank you. But I still have a little money of my own."

"The second secretary's orders are definite. You are to take everything he has given you."

Munpa bowed. "Please thank him on my behalf, also for sending the doctor, the treatment, the hospitality . . . you have been very good to me here."

The gatekeeper made no reply. Evidently neither the secretary nor the abbot had expressed a desire to see Munpa before he left.

The course of events had come full turn. Once again Munpa was out in the street, but he was better equipped now. He had more money and an extra robe, and his back had healed.

Munpa felt tremendously relieved. The silence of the monastery had oppressed him, and the elaborate manifestations on his cell wall were incomprehensible to his untrained brain. The Zen master had wanted to teach him that the world is no more than a play of images, rising up in one's mind, escaping for a while, only to be swallowed back into their source in time. Munpa hadn't understood. Unable to accept that the whitewashed walls of his cell contained no more than his own projections, frightened, in fact, by his own mind, Munpa ran away.

THIS TIME HE welcomed the city's turmoil and strode through street after street, smiling pleasantly. No more lukewarm rice and tasteless cabbage; he would eat well again. He crossed the bridge and hailed a rickshaw. He grinned as he watched cobblestones and sidewalks flashing past. How pleasant it was to be away from the bewitched walls where a sorcerer manipulated the scenery. He waited until he spotted a good restaurant and told the coolie to stop. He paid the man with the remaining coppers from the hochan's change. When he jumped down, his back didn't hurt. He had forgotten both jail and judge — how could he, a Tibetan, have been beaten by Chinese constables?

A servile waiter showed him in, and Munpa ordered a plate of his favorite momos and a large bowl of noodles.

"Anything to drink?"

"A jug."

"Large or small?"

"Large. This is a special occasion."

Yellow Hat monks are not allowed to drink alcohol, but even the strict gelugspas tend to forget the rule as soon as they are a safe distance from their monasteries. The Chinese rice wine made Munpa's blood glow and accelerated his digestion. He ordered more momos. The waiter, puzzled by the agitated foreigner's appetite, suggested a cash payment. He was reassured when Munpa put some silver on the table.

Munpa burped happily, and gradually his mind relaxed. He began to consider the future again. He waited for his change, tipped the waiter liberally, and left the restaurant. It would be a good idea to retrieve his possessions. He still had a blanket and a leather bag half full of provisions stored at the caravansary.

He arrived as a large caravan was filing into the inn's vast court. It was soon followed by another. The innkeeper and his assistants were running about. Munpa bowed.

"Good day, Mr. Chao."

The Chinese stopped and smiled. "My Tibetan friend, what a timely arrival! Give us a hand, please. We have to unload the mules and keep them apart. The Urga mules go over there, and the ones from Kashgar will have the southern stable. Ask the merchants to tell you which animal is which. We musn't get them mixed up. We'll water them later when we have some room in the court."

Munpa set to work at once. The alcohol had lost its effect already and the good food supplied him with ample energy. Within an hour calm reigned once again in the caravansary. The mules had drunk their fill and were eating, and even the camels, directed to the second court, seemed well tempered. Dinner was served. Some of the merchants were smoking opium; others drank tea and talked quietly to each other.

Chao invited Munpa to a meal of mutton. "You've been away a long time. Any luck in catching your thief?"

Munpa shook his head. "No."

Chao understood, from the shortness of the answer and Munpa's expression, that there wasn't any point in asking more questions. He nodded and began to think about other matters. Chao wasn't only an innkeeper, he was a merchant in his own right and the buyer of some of the goods that the merchants from Mongolia had brought in that day. He got up, gave Munpa his blanket and provisions, and invited him to stay the night. "You can sleep in one of the stable lofts if you like. There'll be no charge. You did good work just now."

Munpa stayed on. The camels had been taken to the hills to graze, but the mules needed attention. Munpa worked in the stables again, ate free meals, and made some money on tips. He didn't particularly want to leave, as the routine suited him. If Lobsang had ever been in the city he would surely have left by now. The turquoise? Only a miracle could retrieve it. Miracles arrive at the right time. It wasn't that he had lost faith, but he preferred to wait for the miracle than try to chase after it again.

The memory of the walls in his cell at Supreme Serenity still haunted him. He remembered that he had been shown a caravan complete with mules, camels, and merchants on horseback. And he himself had been there too, traveling somewhere. It is true that he had thought the caravan part of the Zen guru's manipulation, a trick to catch his spirit, but now a new idea crossed Munpa's mind. Couldn't that mysterious miniature caravan have been some indication, a hint? Would he perhaps be traveling with such a caravan one day?

The conflict between his desire to serve Gyalwai Odzer and to remain where he was lost its urgency. He told himself that he probably couldn't stay in the inn for any length of time, but meanwhile there were the good meals, Chao's friendly company, and the work he was accustomed to. He preferred to wait until something happened.

Something did happen: a new impulse nudged the unwilling Munpa. A merchant from Kashgar told him that his caravan would soon be leaving. "We are shorthanded and could use a good man like yourself. You don't have to come all the way. Some of my men will be waiting for me further along. Let's say you'll have work until we reach Kan-chou, or perhaps Su-chou."

Munpa had a vague idea where these cities were situated, because some of his kinsmen had been that way. He remembered that everything was supposed to be made of stone in those parts: khangs, furniture, kitchenware, anything, and recalled having owned a Su-chou stone plate, of a rather lovely color, a pale gray, almost mauve. Both cities are well placed on the western route and attract much business. Perhaps Lobsang had gone to one of them in the hope of finding the right customer for the jewel. From a Tibetan point of view, the cities were remote and well situated to hide a foreign criminal.

The merchant's invitation was clearly a sign, and after some deliberation Munpa accepted his offer.

The caravan included a large number of camels and mules, which provided much work: each evening when the caravan reached an inn and each morning when they had to be loaded and prodded into another day's march. When there were no inns, camps had to be made, and guarded, for the merchants carried valuable goods and robbers were said to roam in the plains and hills. The merchants and their assistants were heavily armed. The caravan moved slowly, regulating its speed according to the camels' leisurely progress. The men talked a Turkestan dialect that Munpa didn't understand. Left to his own company, he observed the landscape, guarded the animals, and pondered his fate.

In Kan-chou the caravan halted and spent two days, gathering strength to enter the Gobi. On the threshold of the forbidding desert no one seemed in a hurry to break camp.

Munpa, used to Tibet's semideserts whose rocky ground

usually grows some weeds or brush, was surprised by the flowing sands that stretched to the horizon. The ground was yellow, sometimes blackish. Occasional short bursts of wind enveloped the travelers in clouds of brittle sand. He could see them approach, but there was nowhere to hide. The moving walls swept down on the unfortunate caravan, choking and hurting man and beast alike. The camels plodded on, but the mules panicked, lost their loads, ran off, and had to be caught.

The inns sold water, dirty and with a foul taste. Even Munpa's hardy stomach had trouble holding it, but he tried not to vomit. He would be thirsty again and the supply was limited.

High watchtowers marked the route at regular distances. Most of them were ruined by age and neglect, like the high wall that connected them and that, in places, had degenerated into an immense line of rubble.

Munpa pointed, and looked at one of the muleteers.

"What is that?"

"The Great Wall."

"What does it enclose?"

"China," said the muleteer.

Munpa walked on dreamily.

*

When they reached Su-chou, Munpa was disappointed. The beautiful stoneware he had heard so much about turned out to be no more than some bowls and vases of indifferent quality, displayed in a few stores. The city was like all the other Chinese towns he had seen, fairly small, crowded, and noisy. Would Lobsang have traveled as far as Su-chou? Munpa didn't think so. Should he continue? The sign he had thought he would find at Su-chou did not exist. He again began to torture himself with conflicting thoughts.

The merchants thanked him. They had enough help now and Munpa's services were no longer required. After they paid him, the caravan took three days to reorganize itself before trundling on into the sands.

Munpa watched its departure: men and mules formed a compact mass dominated by the camels in their middle. Its outline faded slowly, and the caravan became a vague dark shape, diminishing slowly in the yellow waste of the desert. Munpa could still discern the camels, but they too finally faded away. A moving point, closer and closer to the horizon. Then nothing.

The distressed Munpa felt lonely for the first time in his life. He was lost in a void. The desert of endless sand could not be compared to the familiar wilderness of the Chang Tang, where he knew the lay of the land, recognized the mountains, and felt close to his kinsmen living in scattered camps. Shivers ran up and down his body; his head ached. The fever increased when he returned to the inn. He stretched out on the khang and listened to the silence left by his companions.

That afternoon his condition worsened. His bones were cold, but his head burned. The fatigue caused by traveling through alien lands, the bad water he had drunk, the worry that had slipped back into his mind all combined to undermine his strength. He could think of nothing he wanted to do. Why travel farther? But to return alone through the desert seemed as laborious as going on.

The innkeeper came in to ask his guest if there was anything he wanted. Was Munpa waiting for other travelers? More caravans would be due to arrive soon. Where did his guest want to go?

Munpa had no idea. He was tired and ill and wanted to rest.

His host nodded, "You don't look well at all. Please come

with me. I have another room, nice and quiet, farther away from the courtyard. You should eat. I will send you some soup."

Munpa thanked the innkeeper and tried to eat but felt nauseated and pushed the bowl away. He slept heavily, dreaming of horrors that he couldn't remember when he woke. His head still hurt, and the slightest sound sent red-hot tremors cutting through his skull. The innkeeper came to suggest he consult a doctor, but Munpa refused. He would be all right the next day. The next day he felt worse.

A caravan arrived, and the animals' snorting, whinnying, and balking replaced the silence of the desert. Men shouted and buckets clashed. The innkeeper, a man of unusual compassion, worried about his sick guest.

"You cannot travel in the state you're in. You'll need at least a week to recover. In an inn like this you're not comfortable. My sister-in-law owns a large house, and she'll be pleased to rent you a room where nothing will bother you. I often send her guests when the inn is full. You can eat at her house. She's in business and has many servants. If you like I'll let her know that you're here."

Munpa agreed, but he enquired about the price.

"You'll pay less than what we charge here."

Within two hours Munpa found himself in a room in a Chinese-style house, with a view of the first courtyard. The room's luxurious furniture proclaimed the lady's wealth. He hadn't seen her yet. The servants said she was busy but would meet him the next day. Munpa didn't care. He only wanted to lie down and sleep.

It seemed that rest was all he needed. For ten days he did little else but sleep and eat the thin rice gruel the lady's servants brought him. The good lady was treating her patient in the Chinese manner. Tibetans feed their sick with great quantities of their choicest foods; the Chinese believe in fasting. The tasteless gruel reminded Munpa of his days in the temple of Supreme Serenity, but while his bowels rumbled unhappily the fever ebbed away and his head began to feel normal again. Losing weight improved his appearance, and the *némo*, the lady of the house, was quick to notice that her guest was quite a handsome young man. She observed the tall, attractive Tibetan sunning himself in her courtyard and invited him into her living quarters.

Munpa never told her he was a monk. He hadn't told his traveling companions either. Most of the Tibetan clergy, including the venerable priests of high standing, prefer to be incognito while traveling so as not to be hindered by the rules of chastity and sobriety. Munpa was no exception. Like all Tibetans he liked to drink, and he didn't deny himself any sexual pleasure if it happened to be available. The némo was a lovely woman.

Nénuphar had just turned thirty when Munpa met her, and their attraction was mutual. He liked her stately, well-shaped body, which contrasted with the slight Chinese women around her and betrayed her Mongolian ancestors. But she was part Chinese too and had inherited some of that race's characteristics. Nénuphar was a practical woman and knew how to run the commercial empire left by her husband who had died three years ago. The lady had been busy since then, and happy being in charge. Now, however, with the handsome foreigner in her house, she became aware of a certain lack in her life. But sex would never be the némo's main concern. She defined it as a purely physical activity, pleasurable during breaks from more serious occupations.

Nénuphar, already a wealthy woman, meant to increase her possessions. The penniless foreigner would not be a suitable match. But she enjoyed Munpa's company and was pleased when he didn't object to working. It's good to have a strong and honest man around when goods and silver change hands or caravans are loaded with expensive merchandise. Her business was growing. There was even more to do, and she couldn't be everywhere at once.

"Ah . . ." the némo said to herself, and left it at that, unwilling to analyze her feelings too deeply. She welcomed the accommodating Munpa to her table and bed, desirous of investigating his exotic lovemaking.

Munpa was the second man she had met on intimate terms. She had been a faithful wife and Munpa was the first interesting male who had presented himself since the death of her spouse.

Munpa accepted the situation as a matter of course, showing no extreme enthusiasm, and events developed and connected in an easy, logical manner.

*

Life flowed on. Munpa, free of fever and pain, became active again, but his mind was still depressed. He no longer felt the zeal that had accompanied the early stages of his quest. The herdsman isn't used to planning too far ahead. The people of the Chang Tang can track a lost animal, occasionally partake in hunting, and enjoy a little warfare from time to time, but they aren't sleuths capable of pursuing a wily criminal. Munpa's further training as a monk and an attendant to a guru hadn't equipped him for the present task. He now felt unable to make any further effort and was unwilling to even think about Lobsang and the turquoise. Hadn't he tried everything already? He began to admit that he might have misread the miraculous signs, and at despondent moments he even doubted their very existence. When there was nothing to do he would wander about the house and its courts or stand staring for long moments without thinking of anything in particular.

His relation with the némo, whom he now addressed by

75

her first name, failed to uplift his mood, and he performed his intimate duties in such a distracted manner that he vexed his partner. That Munpa hardly ever listened to her conversation was another negative factor that displeased Nénuphar. Thinking that Chinese food might not stimulate her foreign lover she spoke to her cook. Munpa enjoyed the enormous chunks of broiled meat and the noodle soup, thick with tsampa and seasoned soda, and appreciated being served beer and strong liquor. He understood the heavy hint and tried to improve his performance.

His lack of enthusiasm persisted, however, and he began to prefer his mistress' Chinese meals, for he knew that nothing would be expected of him if the table was covered with small dishes containing the subtle delicacies that all Chinese crave. The némo was disappointed but preferred not to complain openly, reasoning that some pleasure was better than none. Munpa felt vaguely guilty. He also felt bored.

His special position required him to supervise the servants and take an active part in Nénuphar's major business dealings but these duties did not improve his mood either. Since the némo never paid him for his work he considered himself a bargain. The more be became convinced that he was wasting his time and energy the more he looked forward to leaving Su-chou. But where would he go? And what would he do if he reached another place? The urge to depart increased when he, hidden by stacked bales of hay, overheard a conversation between two servants.

"The némo is going to send a caravan to Sinkiang," one servant said. "The Tibetan will be in charge."

"A lot of good that'll do him," the other retorted. "The poor bastard will be eating desert sand and choke in his tent during the days. It's too hot now for normal travel. Caravans can move only by night. Some trip that'll be! I've done it twice now, and I'll never do it again if I can help it."

"You're right. I've done it too, but I had some good company that time. All he'll have is half a dozen Huie-Huie, and those cutthroats from Turkestan gabble their own lingo. He'll never understand a word they say."

The other servant cursed. "Huie-Huie! I can't stand them. They're short-tempered at the best of times, and this time they'll have a reason since he'll be the boss. They like to steal, you know."

The first servant laughed. "Traveling with Huie-Huie through a hot desert. He might as well go to the lower hells for a spell. I hope he'll make some money on the deal."

"Forget it. You know how stingy the némo is. She beds with him, doesn't she? That's all he'll ever get out of her."

"You think they'll marry in the end?"

"Not on your life. She's proud too. He's a savage, a herdsman from some weird country no decent person has ever heard of. Don't you know that he came as a muleteer's assistant hanging on to some caravan from Lan-chou? All he owns are the clothes on his back. The némo's husband was an important trader, and so were his father and grandfather. Our lady will never share her gold with a tramp who happened to stumble into her house."

"So why did she jump into bed with him and why is he still around?"

"Bah! Women are like rabbits. They have no brains. You can never figure out what they'll do next."

"I think I can figure it out. He's a giant, and she's big too. She wants things to fit."

"Ha! Right! But that's no reason to marry, you know."

The men left the warehouse, and Munpa was left to ponder the import of their discussion. He wasn't surprised, for he knew that he had kindled no real passion in Nénuphar's heart. He hadn't wanted to either. He had been no more than a partner in the némo's game. The gossiping ser-

77

vants made it clear to him that he had been losing the game.

So he would go, but he didn't want to flee the house like some despicable vagrant. He would tell Nénuphar that he was leaving, buy some provisions with money, not love-making, and get out of Su-chou. Once he had liberated himself from her power, he would decide what direction to take.

*

For several days Munpa wandered about the némo's house. Thinking about his decision to leave Su-chou, he was reminded of his escape from the monastery Supreme Serenity. Once again he had forgotten his promise to Gyalwai Odzer, whose body was still waiting for the return of the turquoise. His guilt grew when he realized how much time had passed since he had left the hermitage. At least a year had gone by, maybe two years. How could he keep track of time; so much had happened since that horrible discovery.

Other thoughts bothered him too. Had he really left that small cell in the Zen temple? Couldn't it be that he was still there, that his mind was still caught in that swirling world in miniature, where a trapa joined a caravan of merchants, with camels swaying in an endless desert of sterile, flowing sand?

The wall's prediction was explicit enough. Many of the images showed what had then been future and had now joined the past. The Great Wall of China — hadn't he seen that too, in between meals of rice and cabbage in the silent cell? Why did he have to bother to live through it all if the details of his life were fixed anyway in the imaginative spells of that wicked little abbot?

He left the house and walked into town. His fear subsided and he began to smile. He was in a drawing, on the wall of a monk's cell, and everything else was too. Amusing, very. A bizarre spectacle. Why should only his own life be fixed? Had he discovered, perchance, a general rule? No doubt he would meet with Lobsang in the end, capture the turquoise, return it to Gyalwai Odzer, whom he had seen meditating in another wall picture. Yes, Odzer was there too. Everybody was.

He smiled again. *"The world is nothing but a series of pictures, painted on a wall."* Odzer himself had said that, but not to Munpa. He had been talking to advanced disciples, capable of grasping his words. Munpa shrugged. So perhaps he could understand some of the hermit's teaching too now.

He tried to reason a little further. He had *entered* the pictures; he must have, for he had been part of the caravan and other scenes. How does one get into anything? Through some opening, of course, a door, a window, a crack in the rocks, a hole in a wall. He had heard tales of great saints, living incarnations, passing through walls, mountains, and other obstacles. But however these *doubtobs* managed their miracles, they must have slipped through some particular point. Munpa couldn't remember when and how he had penetrated the wall. He had forgotten — how annoying. He could have been pushed too, by the abbot, for instance. He didn't remember being pushed either.

This existence of some opening, never mind how small, was of extreme importance. One enters a room through a door, one leaves through the same door. If he could find the opening he would be able to liberate himself. But wasn't it strange that he had forgotten how he got in? The moment, after all, was of supreme importance. He wouldn't want to forget it. So some superior force had *made* him forget it.

As he walked through Su-chou he studied doors and windows. He opened a gate and looked at the garden behind it. Interesting, but the garden was still in the wall. A little further along he leaned on a fence and contemplated the desert. The desert was in the wall too. Everything he could experience through his senses had to be part of the same illusion. "*The world is nothing but a series of pictures, painted on a wall.*" It was amazing that he hadn't grasped this truth before. But to understand wasn't enough. He wanted to get out, to be free.

The next day he walked back into town, didn't look where he was going, and bumped into two Taoists, dressed in blue robes, their long hair stuck up in knots. Munpa excused himself, walked on, but turned around. He knew that Taoists specialize in supernatural wisdom and are able to predict the future. Strange that he would meet these sages at such a meaningful moment. Could this be the next sign? He stopped. The Taoists, surprised to see a Tibetan such a distance from "the roof of the world," looked around too. Munpa bowed and asked the two Chinese if they would be good enough to perform a *mo* for him, adding that he needed the soothsaying ceremony as he was about to leave on a journey.

"Where to?"

"Ah, that's just the point. I don't know the goal of my journey." Munpa clinked some silver in the pocket of his robe.

The Taoists smiled. "Certainly. There's a place of worship nearby. The street is not an appropriate place for a *mo*."

They turned into a side street and found the temple, a small building containing several statues. The Taoists sat down on some steps leading to an altar on which an old man sat on a throne. The old man had been hewn out of stone and had a long beard and lifelike eyes. He smiled down on Munpa, who immediately liked the god. He wondered what method the Taoists would use? Would they throw beans on a checkerboard and then add the figures indicated on each square to find the right page in a book filled with predictions? Or would they use dice, juggle bones, or prepare an evil-smelling brew to study the movement of small objects floating on its surface?

"State your question."

"Where shall I go when I leave Su-chou?"

The Taoists nodded and busied themselves. Munpa had already paid them a sizable fee, and the soothsayers mumbled ferociously to deepen their concentration. The beans slid to their places on the board and the Taoists consulted their books. They drew together, comparing notes. Finally one of them got up and spoke solemnly: "You will have to follow the sun."

Munpa repeated the answer but didn't seem to understand. The caretaker of the temple, a portly little fellow, spoke up in a high voice: "The sun rises in the east and sinks in the west, the oracle wants you to go west."

"True," the Taoists said pleasantly. "West."

The caretaker had heard silver pass hands and wasn't going to let go of Munpa so easily. "The answer is clear, of course, sir, but you may need further advice. This is a Taoist temple and our saints are immortals. It so happens that a true immortal spends his time in meditation in a pavilion at the end of our temple garden."

"Really?" Munpa asked politely.

"And I am the immortal's attendant," the small fat man said happily. "But the immortal may not wish to see you, although I will pass your request if you so desire."

Munpa hesitated.

The attendant pointed at the statue on the altar. "You can also ask *him*."

"How?"

"Use this vase. It contains bamboo tablets. Each one has a number. Shake it and turn it upside-down. The first tablet to fall out will guide us to a page in this book. You will have an answer."

He held up his hand and Munpa dropped some coins

into its demanding palm. He shook the vase clumsily. The attendant read the number on the first of the tablets that clattered on the stone floor and consulted his book.

"The answer is complicated. You are surrounded by beings of different, even opposing, natures. It will be difficult for you to pursue a favorable course."

Munpa sighed and looked at the old god, who was still smiling down at him from the altar.

The attendant bowed. "Perhaps you need the advice of a living immortal. Come back tomorrow morning, and I will be here to tell you whether the sage will see you." He showed his hand again and Munpa lost another few coins.

Munpa returned the next morning and found the attendant waiting for him.

"You are in luck, the *tao-che* will see you. Don't offer him any money, because you will insult him if you do. He has no use for money. If you wish to pay you can pay me, since I am charged with buying provisions for the temple. You can offer the sage some fruit, flowers, and incense. Did you bring a gift of that nature?"

"No."

"Come with me. I may have just what you need."

Munpa bought the offerings and was taken into the garden. He admired the elegant lines of a small pavillion set among flowering shrubs. The old man he found within, sitting in the lotus position on a square hard cushion, resembled the god on the altar. Munpa was also reminded of the abbot of Supreme Serenity. Was he to be involved in more magic? Would the tao-che be like the Zen master and communicate without words?

But the tao-che spoke at once.

"Sit down. What bothers you? Why are you traveling so far from your country? You are a Tibetan, what business brings you to China? Are you a merchant?"

Munpa breathed easily. These were acceptable questions,

pertaining to a familiar reality. But he was still nervous, would this "Venerable Celestial" suddenly withdraw from the interview by "looking within"? The sage looked straight into Munpa's eyes. "Well?"

"I am following a thief," Munpa said.

"What did he take from you?"

"He took a reliquary from my teacher."

"Did your teacher order you to pursue the thief?"

Munpa restrained a groan.

"Where exactly does your teacher live?"

"In the province of Tsinghai."

"Is there any particular reason to suspect that the thief may be here in Su-chou or in this part of the country? Why have you been sent here?"

Munpa remained silent.

The tao-che's mood changed. "Is this tale true? It seems to me that you are inventing some sort of story. Why?" His tone of voice became sharp, almost menacing. "I didn't call you. I don't care about your business. You wanted to see me. Why are you telling this lie?"

Munpa began to stutter. "I . . . I'm sorry, sir. I did not want to offend you. My mind is confused . . . I don't know what to do anymore . . . where to go."

"Go back to your teacher. Tell him you couldn't find the reliquary. Thieves often go free. China is vast — the fellow can be hiding in a million places."

"My very saintly master is dead," Munpa whispered. Again he began to shiver from head to foot. Was Gyalwai Odzer really dead?

"He is dead," the tao-che said. "So what happened? Did you leave immediately after the funeral? What has been done with his body? I believe you people burn the dead or leave them somewhere so that vultures can feed on the corpses." The sage frowned. "A disgusting way of doing things."

83

Munpa felt as if he were being drawn and quartered. "I left at once. There was no time for the funeral rites."

The tao-che thought for a while.

"Listen," he said finally, "I can feel that you do not want to tell me what really happened. It doesn't matter anyway. But know this: each of us has ten souls, three *houen*, of a superior nature, and seven *p'o*, which are much inferior. At death the ten souls disconnect and each follows its separate way, according to its allotted time span. In the end, they all dissolve into their source to become part of the unformed again.

"Some sages, those who practice the spiritual disciplines correctly, reach the state of *chen jen*, the truly free, and become immortals. The sages fulfill the human purpose, but most men allow themselves to become sidetracked and die before they have been able to liberate themselves, having wasted the number of years allotted to them. Their inferior souls, the seven p'o, remain attracted to the rotting physical corpse and float around cemeteries. The three superior souls, the houen, unable to reach the level of immortality, are taken to the heavenly court and judged by the ten magistrates, who decide how long each of them will have to exist in pleasant or unpleasant spheres, depending on the original individual's deeds during his life on earth."

Munpa knew that each human being will live a certain number of years and that the duration of the period is predetermined. He hadn't understood the tao-che's discourse very well, but this point about "a number of years" made some impression.

"Could it be that this number of years is cut short by an accident causing the death of the individual?"

The tao-che looked up. "*What?* You mean to say that your master didn't die of old age or some illness?"

"My teacher was murdered." The answer escaped from him. Munpa hadn't wanted to tell the tao-che.

"Murdered?! And *you* killed him?"

"No! no! Not me!" Munpa jumped up. "Never!"

"All right. So you're after the murderer." The tao-che smiled, relieved that he wasn't facing a killer.

Munpa gestured frantically. "But things . . . demons perhaps . . . are all around me. I don't know where I am anymore, yet I have to keep going. But where to? My life is like a mad dream now."

"Calm yourself. Possibly your master has become an immortal. If he hasn't, his superior souls will be wandering about somewhere, here on earth probably, separated from his dead body, waiting for the predestined number of years of his normal life to come to an end. Your guru may be advanced, in which case his three houen will be sympathetic to your cause. The inferior souls, however . . ."

The tao-che took a deep breath. "I'll ask you once more. Was the body burned or buried? What is the custom in your part of Tibet?"

"I . . . I left the body on its cushions and prepared some offerings. Then I went away. There was no time to lose. My teacher lived by himself, in a cave. It may have been months before his death became known. Maybe his body is still in the hermitage."

"Right!" the tao-che shouted. "Of course! The seven inferior souls turned into demons. Some of them have been following you and are causing trouble now by confusing your thoughts. They are responsible for any unpleasant events that may have occurred. But one of the superior souls must be with you too, for you have traveled far and you are still safe and sound."

The tao-che straightened his back, took a deep breath, and became silent. Munpa waited. Would the sage give him some advice now? Suddenly the old man shivered and seemed to pull himself free from a state of deep reflection. He looked at Munpa as if he had never seen his visitor before and made an impatient gesture. "Very well. You have been told. On your way now!"

He got up and disappeared through a door in the back of the little room.

Munpa looked at the empty seat for a while. A hand nudged his sleeve and he saw the attendant standing next to him.

Together they walked back to the temple's main building.

MUNPA LEANED AGAINST one of the portals of the temple's main door. The tao-che's words still reverberated in his head. People wanting to visit the temple pushed past his hulking body, and he reluctantly left, walking slowly to Nénuphar's house.

Multiple souls separating after an individual's death. The idea wasn't all that far-fetched. Tibetans have a similar theory, although they name the souls differently. He remembered that different *tulkus,* or aspects of the Buddha-nature, may incarnate in the same lama, dominating his mind, speech, and body. Other souls again are in charge of the senses. But he knew nothing about what would happen to these different entities after death. In Odzer's case some of them might have followed Munpa, the way dogs without an owner, roaming about in the desert, attach themselves to any traveler. Isn't it true that wandering demons grab hold of travelers and follow them into houses? Sometimes people will have nothing to do with unknown visitors, frightened that the man asking for lodging will leave his demons behind when he leaves.

It could very well be that the mishaps of Munpa's journey were caused by Odzer's lower souls, which might, for some reason or other, feel hostile to Munpa. But hadn't the tao-che also said that at least one of the hermit's superior souls would be guarding Munpa's fate?

He let himself into the némo's house and went to his room. That same evening he would announce his departure. He didn't need much time to prepare himself for the journey. All he owned were his thick Tibetan robe, the Chinese robe that had been given to him by the Supreme Serenity's second secretary, his blanket, and a large leather bag to hold his provisions. He would go west as he had been told by the Taoists. Somewhere near the spot where the sun sets the miracle would be waiting for him.

A servant called him for dinner. He was relieved when he saw the Chinese food. No special favors tonight! Thank heaven.

Although Munpa might be an uneducated rustic, he could still display a certain delicacy at times. He wasn't going to enjoy Nénuphar's gourmet cooking if he wasn't able to repay her with his labor. He chose to inform her of his decision before eating, and didn't sit down.

"I'll be leaving in the morning."

The widow wasn't too surprised. Munpa didn't fit in with a Chinese environment, and she had been expecting his departure at some time or other. His lack of interest in her business prevented her from trying to hold on to the Tibetan. He would never be a suitable associate. The affair was over, and they could separate in peace.

"Really? Where do you plan to go?"

"West," Munpa said, pointing vaguely. "And I thank you," he added politely. "You have been very good to me." He referred to her hospitality. The rest didn't matter, a little activity on the side . . . he had forgotten already.

Nénuphar understood, although she preferred not to. "West," she repeated. "Right. Tibetans are Buddhists, are they not? You will be going on a pilgrimage, to Tun-huang, of course, the holy abode of the thousand Buddhas."

Munpa gasped. Another sign, at last! He began to shiver with sudden agitation. He had never heard about this holy place. No doubt it would be a source of miracles. He no longer doubted that one of the hermit's better souls was taking an active interest in his well-being.

As Munpa wasn't saying anything, Nénuphar believed that she had guessed right.

"I will give you a good supply of food and utensils. You'll need a big water container. You'll be in the desert, and you shouldn't forget to fill it whenever there is an opportunity. Maybe I should lend you a mule so that you won't have to exhaust yourself carrying your baggage. You can return the mule on your way back."

The idea of returning didn't appeal to Munpa. "Thank you, but a true pilgrim travels on foot. I will gladly accept the food, but I will pay you. I have some silver."

"You won't pay me anything," the némo stated firmly. "Please do not insult me. You have been useful to me, so the provisions will be your wages. I will also give you some incense, to be burned in honor of the Buddhas of Tun-huang. Tell them that Nénuphar pays her respects."

Munpa grumbled quietly to himself. "A few provisions in the way of wages! I haven't exactly made a fortune here. What about my other services? Why does she keep on saying that she is *giving* . . . ?" But he made an effort to smile and ate the Chinese food that he still hadn't learned to appreciate. Everything had been said.

When the meal was over, Nénuphar didn't hint at a passionate farewell and Munpa scampered off to the privacy of his own khang. His mind was at peace; the superior part of Gyalwai's spirit would continue to take care of him. He lay down and fell asleep at once.

*

The next morning a servant brought him his leather bag and Munpa checked its contents. The lady had outdone herself. Apart from an ample supply of food he found some utensils, a good-quality water bottle, and a pair of excellent leather boots. He repacked the bag, said goodbye, and strode out of the house. It didn't take long before the western trail stretched ahead, as yellow and dusty as the desert itself. Contemplating the land of agony all around, he wished that he had waited for a caravan. He felt loneliness gnawing at his vitals as he forced himself to continue, and tried to think of the thousand Buddhas waiting at the end of the journey. The image slipped away. There was nothing to see in this hostile land except the remnants of the Great Wall, a ragged line in the north, a long stretch of rubble broken, here and there, by crumbling towers, still trying to protect China against foreign warriors and fierce demons.

From time to time he passed what was left of houses and farms and even the remnants of entire villages, abandoned and in ruins. Walls and roofs might still be intact, but all salvageable materials had disappeared a long time ago. Not a single door, window, or board remained. He wondered why the inhabitants had fled. The sand had forced them out no doubt; the persistent particles patiently blew into fields and homes, until all life was stifled. Some of the wells contained a little water, dirty and of a vile taste. He didn't appreciate the beauty of the smoothly flowing dunes that remained as victors, pushing the ruins gently until, some time soon, the last traces of human habitation would be obliterated completely.

The nightmarish landscape tired him and slowed his step.

An inn appeared that first evening. It consisted of a small courtyard and a low building with a single khang, filling the entire back of the house. Munpa was the only visitor.

"Did you bring any food?" the innkeeper asked. "If not, I can cook up something."

"Just some hot water, please."

Munpa climbed the khang, sat down, and studied the contents of his bag again. Nénuphar had done a good job, but the bag was heavy. There was no reason to complain about its weight, as he had enough food to last him a good while and the load would lessen day by day. He picked up the various items. Several large round loaves of bread, a good supply of flour, salted pork, three smoked ducks, packages of dry noodles, condiments, dried mushrooms, tea, salt, a can of lard, another of soy sauce. Nénuphar had also considered the fact that he would have to cook his meals and included a small metal pot, an enamel mug, and a pair of chopsticks. His mood improved; to have enough to eat is the prime concern of any Tibetan. He would ration himself with care and eat the bread first. It would be enough for several days, and afterward he could bake more. Right now he would just have some tea. He repacked the bag, prepared a large bowl of strong tea, and stretched out on the warm tiles of the khang, using his bag as a pillow.

The next morning he jumped down and looked out the door. The naked yellow desert awaited him again, an endless forbidding space without a single feature to please the eye. Country of demons indeed!

"How do you stand living out here?" he asked the innkeeper, who was pouring boiling water into his bowl.

"I don't. I'll be leaving soon. The sand is pushing me out, just as it did the others."

"Which others?"

"The villagers. There used to be quite a few houses out here, fields, wells — we were doing well. We built walls to defend ourselves against the desert, but we couldn't keep it out. Each day, each night, the sand piled up, pushing, destroying. Three years ago most of the villagers left. Come."

He pointed out the door. "That hill over there hides a large farmhouse. The owner stayed on as long as he could but he left too, last year that was. This inn will be another hill. I don't have more than another year or so. The well will be filled in, and what good is an inn without water?"

"The place is cursed!" Munpa exclaimed. "What have you people done that you deserve such a cruel fate?"

"No idea. The old men of the village would say that their fathers already knew the desert would destroy us. A hundred years ago this was fertile country. Wise men from Peking have been here and dug holes. They say they found the remains of great cities, temples, even beautiful statues of Buddha. I've seen some myself. But the Gobi came and swallowed it all . . . Are you a follower of Buddha?"

"Certainly," Munpa said. "I'm a pilgrim on my way to visit the abode of the thousand Buddhas."

"Ah! You mean near the town of Tun-huang? I have never been there, but they say it is a very holy place. There are caves containing so many images that nobody has ever been able to count them, because if you try they keep on multiplying."

"Amazing!" Munpa said happily. "But it's still far. I wish I were there already. How long do pilgrims usually take to get there?"

"It depends on how the traveler experiences the distance. It's not merely a matter of counting miles, you see. When you are tired or weak it will take long, but if your faith carries you you'll hardly notice the time." The inn-keeper watched Munpa tear off a duck's leg. "You seem to be a strong man, sir, and well supplied. Your journey will take several days, certainly no more than a week."

*

In spite of the enthusiasm Munpa felt about the Buddhas he was about to meet — the observance of a religious image

means more for a Tibetan than the simple act of seeing it —
the dreary landscape soon depressed him again. His bag
weighed more than it should. His pace slackened and each
step involved a separate decision. There was no inn waiting
for him at the end of the day and he slept in the sand, near
the ruins of another village. He was lucky that he was traveling in the spring. In winter temperatures drop to well be-
low zero and the desert kills many weary voyagers, freezing
them inside their bedrolls, and during summer the traveler
may die of thirst and sunstroke. Munpa could rest quietly,
however, with the sand building up against the side of his
body.

He woke stiff all over and his hands trembled. Surely
the fever hadn't come back already? He worried about his
health as he walked away. He had never been ill in his life,
except in this damned country where evil spirits assailed him
constantly. He wished he had never left the Chang Tang.
Who had ever seen anything like this land, buried, wiped
away, monotonous, spreading out in every direction?

Homesickness gripped his mind. The little monastery,
the quiet cave, relatives and friends, the animals of the Tibetan highlands, mountain ranges, all sorts of well-known
and loved images filled his mind. And there was always
Gyalwai Odzer, the guru he had served so well.

Sentences taken from Milarepa's hymns, sung by the
advanced disciples of the hermit, joined to make up an im-
provised prayer:

Oh, my master, incarnated Buddha
For whom even the gods bow down,
Refuge of all beings,
Listen to the prayer of the solitary pilgrim.
I call you in my misery
Grant me your grace
Bless me with the vision of your divine face.

I am here to serve you,
Lost in this unknown and hostile land.
Look at me from the invisible sojourn where you are.

Munpa had lifted his folded hands in an adoring gesture, and tears trickled down his haggard face, leaving traces on his cheeks streaked with sand. He prostrated himself and pressed his face into the ground, in a culmination of patient devotion.

No vision resulted. He didn't feel the blissful touch of his guru's hands on his head. When he got up, the trail still stretched ahead and the desert was as dead as before. Why did Gyalwai Odzer refuse to help him? It was his own fault; he hadn't retrieved the turquoise the hermit was waiting for.

Or, horror of horrors, could it be that the long separation between the master and the turquoise would explain Odzer's failing strength? The hermit had projected his form, illuminating the night with its splendor when Munpa begged for help before. But now he could not. The villainous Lobsang hadn't been able to kill the master's inner essence when he hit him with the bronze kettle. Perhaps only now the murder was effectively accomplished.

Munpa screamed with fear. What could he do? It was unlikely that he would run into Lobsang in this miserable desert. But there was still the miracle, announced by the soothsayers and the tao-che. "Go west." He was going west. "The superior part of your teacher is protecting you." So it was. He was still alive, approaching the thousand Buddhas. He was a Buddhist. A thousand Buddhas would be sure to help and guide him to the turquoise.

Intermittent attacks of fever slowed his progress, and the daily marches became shorter. One day he could hardly get up at all and he shivered in semiconsciousness between two heaps of sand. He found water from time to time, in neglected and stinking wells, but it was bitter and burned his stomach.

"Soon you will have to turn south," an innkeeper told him. "If you don't you will go on and reach the great Jade Gate."

"Gate to where?"

"Gate *from* where," the Chinese innkeeper said curtly.

"I'll be out of China?"

"Of course. Sinkiang is Chinese, the barbarians live in the west. You'll be in Russia."

Munpa had heard of Russia but doubted its existence. As a Tibetan he only acknowledged Tibet, China, and India, and that faraway place where the blue-eyed demons live. Some of them had penetrated as far as Lhasa but were forced out again by the supernatural power of the lamas. Or so he had been told — it was all rather vague. Tibet, China, and India were surrounded by the *tchou ter*, a wide sea that cannot be crossed, for the traveler will fall off the earth's rim. So much was clear. He had once seen a puppy dog fall off a table, and this had been his first lesson in geography. A table has a flat top, so has the earth.

"Russia," Munpa said. "That would be close to the great sea, wouldn't it?"

But the innkeeper didn't know about seas, he only knew that Russian Turkestan lies to the west.

Munpa still thought about the great sea.

"How far do you think the sea is from here?"

The innkeeper was pensive. A sea has to do with water; he had seen water in lakes and in the Yellow River. He said he wasn't sure and the conversation came to an end.

Munpa left the inn and struggled on, but the fever weakened him more and more. He sat down at the side of the road and stared at the desert. But was he looking at the desert now or was that really water over there? A lake! Water, to dip his burning face into and to fill his water bottle. It looked so fresh it might not even be bitter.

He got up and ran toward the lake, his feet hardly touching the crusted sand. But he tired soon; the brilliant sun made him sway and he sat down on a low hill, looking down at a depression that might once have been the bed of a brook.

The miracle was happening! The lake stretched from his feet as far as he could see, its color a pure blue, of the same superb transparency as the waters of his homeland. Munpa sat and gazed, forgetting the misery of his long pilgrimage, bathing his tired senses in the fresh atmosphere of the alpine air, tasting an inexpressible happiness with every molecule of his body.

There, quite close, the surface of the lake began to ripple, the waters parted, and a nâga surged up. Munpa could see the lower part of the water spirit's body, appearing as delicate lines of glistening scales, changing their colors continuously. Its upper half was humanlike in shape and supported a head that smiled with compassion.

"Munpa," the nâga said, "your constant devotion to your master deserves a reward. You will receive it now. Here is the very same turquoise which I gave away once before and which was found again today. Take it and return it to the venerable Gyalwai Odzer, who is waiting for you in the hermitage."

The nâga held up the supernatural gem. The jewel was indeed extraordinary, egg-sized, bluer and more luminous than the sky.

Munpa extended his trembling hand and the talisman dropped into his palm. Then, overcome by emotion, he lost consciousness.

He woke at dawn, lying on a sand heap, his feet resting in a shallow depression. His arms were stretched out and there was something in his clasped right hand. He looked at the pebble.

Mirages occur regularly in the desert and often intensify their apparent reality if the observer is exhausted and feverish. Munpa's tired brain, although familiar with the phenomenon, refused to accept this explanation. This, again, was the work of demons. One or more of the lower souls, as described by the tao-che, had sneaked up to Munpa's sleeping body and managed to exchange his treasure for a worthless pebble.

What could he do to escape these malicious spheres? His master clearly couldn't help him. But soon he would be with the thousand Buddhas. The sooner he got to Tun-huang the better.

While he struggled to his feet, intending to return to the track, he heard somebody laugh. A Chinese stood close by. "You too, eh?"

Munpa, befuddled by his recent experience, nodded. The man laughed even louder. "Don't stay here, friend. Stir yourself! We haven't reached the fence yet. Do you have anyone waiting for you there?"

"I am ill," Munpa whispered. He had no idea what the man was talking about.

"That's bad," the stranger said. "Make an effort all the same. We can go together. If your people aren't waiting for you, my friends can take care of your load. Let's go!"

"Will we be going west?" Munpa asked, worrying about leaving the beaten track.

"Of course. You don't want to go through the checkpoint, do you? Why would you be hiding here then? Is this the first time you've come this way?"

"Yes."

"Poor fellow! If you're new to the game you should never be on your own in this sort of thing, you'll get yourself grabbed. Right, I'll help you, all you have to do is follow me."

Munpa attempted to smile. "You'll be earning yourself some good karma. Assisting a pilgrim on his way brings heavenly reward."

"Ha ha!" The Chinese doubled up with laughter. "'A *pilgrim*' the man says! Some joker you are. But we'll call it a pilgrimage if you insist. Ha ha!" Then he put his finger to his lips. "But maybe we better keep quiet, eh? The desert has ears. We don't want *them* to hear."

Munpa made no attempt to understand what was going on. This man had evidently been sent to help. He thanked his fate as he followed his guide mechanically.

Meanwhile the stranger worked on the details of a plan that had occurred to him when he ran into the lone Tibetan. The man was a smuggler, carrying contraband to Am-hsi. By avoiding the checkpoints of the provincial border he would earn himself a fair sum of money. His accomplices were waiting at the other side and he was in a hurry to meet them at the appointed hour. He had mistaken Munpa, who also possessed a large leather bag, for a fellow smuggler, and the latter's weak physical and mental state inspired him now to refine his strategy. "This fellow is both sick and stupid," the smuggler thought, "or maybe he is a drunk who needs a sip every now and then while he travels. As soon as we get close to the fence I'll make him walk ahead and use him as bait for the soldiers. The frontier is swarming with them these days, and they'll soon show themselves when they see a suspect carrying a sack. I'll be nowhere in sight when the fellow gets himself arrested, and when all is clear I'll make a dash, throw my own bag across the fence to be caught by my friends, and be out of trouble. And if the soldiers aren't around, the idiot can take care of himself and maybe I'll give him something for his troubles."

The smuggler's plan met with success. Munpa did as he

was told and approached the fence by himself. A patrol happened to be in the area.

"Ha! Got you! What do you have in that bag, my man? Wanting to throw it across the fence, were you? An old trick. Let's see what goods you carry!"

"I'm a pilgrim, from Tsinghai, on my way to see the thousand Buddhas."

The soldiers were checking his baggage. "That's right, he is some silly savage. Nothing but food and pots and pans in here, and some very nice boots." He turned to Munpa. "Right. You're not a smuggler, we were mistaken. You must have lost your way; the checkpoint is further along. We'll take you there. The gates will still be closed, but there's an inn where you can rest a bit. We'll be good to you and won't take you to prison, but perhaps you should give us something for our troubles. You don't seem to be needing these boots, for you're not wearing them."

"Take them."

Munpa wondered whether these soldiers really existed. Perhaps this was another hallucination. They might fade away, like the nâga and the turquoise and the lovely lake of the day before. He would be alone again, with nothing but sand all around. But he tied his bag and followed the patrol. The inn wasn't far. The soldiers were already pounding on the door. "Open up! Open up!"

"A pilgrim from Tsinghai, on his way to the abode of the Buddhas, has lost his way."

The soldiers left, joking with each other. Their night had been profitably spent. A few miles away the smuggler congratulated himself on the fruition of his brilliant scheme.

The stars winked down on all this cleverness. Another human comedy: they had seen so many.

Munpa slept peacefully, waking late in the morning. The demons seemed to have lost interest in his existence. A friendly innkeeper served him a good breakfast and served as intermediary to secure his guest a passage to Tun-huang with a caravan that arrived that same day. Before reaching the city a merchant showed him the way to the holy caves.

*

At that time the caves were no longer in use and nobody had taken care of the subterranean temples, that honeycombed several hills, for hundreds of years. The site had once attracted large crowds, eager to be guided through the long corridors adorned with elaborate murals and to seek advice from the adepts in charge of the monastery, where large numbers of monks trained diligently. That the temples were all underground was not caused by a desire to hide, as in the case of the Roman catacombs, where rites were celebrated in secret out of fear of the authorities, or because the masters wished to protect themselves and the teaching from the profane masses. Buddhism has always been a clear religion and does not keep its sanctity to itself. The Buddha taught everybody, and the difference in the receptivity of his audience is the only reason that so many diverging interpretations of his method and sayings developed later.

Various degrees of insight created different sects, colored and influenced by remnants of former religions and local conditions. Of all the Buddhist sects the Nepalese were perhaps the most obscure, and this tainted variation of what had once been a straightforward, though subtle, teaching spread to Tibet. Here again the simple "eightfold path" was forced to absorb much native ritual, especially of the Böns, the sorcerers who had ruled the highlands for many generations by playing on the widely scattered and superstitious local population's fears.

The monks who decorated the caves of Tun-huang, although well away in time from the Buddha's life, were not influenced by the sinister symbolism of latter-day Tantric

Buddhism. Their art is fresh and luminous in the marvelous clear light of Asia, penetrating through many shafts, filtered and reflected by the yellow stone of the hills.

Munpa, suddenly faced by the frescoes, was both dazed and terrified. Reminded of the magic of the walls in his Supreme Serenity monkish cell, he quaked with fear. Wandering from one immense painting to another, he became impressed by the detached quality of Buddhas and Bodhisattvas smiling in transcendent wisdom. Even so his mind was not at rest. Scenes of his own recent past projected themselves and caused a turmoil that was not to be pacified by the endless repetition of beatific imagery.

He began to believe himself to be in the *bardo*, the in-between sphere after death where the spirit is confronted by both demons and gods, each one representing deeds performed in the recently terminated earthly life and the various insights gained during the physical journey. Hadn't he been told that part of the bardo is a desolate desert, where cities lie in ruins, where the hapless traveler is attacked by sandstorms, plagued by hallucinations that change as he approaches, drying out, dying; threatening him instead of sustaining his effort? All that he had seen already. The demons had gone and were replaced by smiling gods. Was he dead now? But he couldn't remember having left his body. They say that a dead man remembers all the details of his life. He *did* remember. He saw the camp where he was born, his parents, the trapas of the little monastery whom he had lived with for a number of years, the disciples of Gyalwai Odzer, and, most clearly of all, the hermit himself. But no single detail of his death came to mind. No last rites, nobody concerning himself with his corpse, no chanting. Surely he would remember having followed the cortege taking his body away, for spirits are said to be compelled to do so. They cannot enter the bardo if they don't. Was he in a more advanced state already, where the spirit begins to forget?

But there is one sure method of determining whether one is alive or dead. The spiritual body leaves no shadow and its feet are turned around.

The experiment was easy enough. Munpa left the corridors and found a spot of clear sunlight on the bank of the little river running close to the caves. He walked about, looking over his shoulder. As it happened to be midday there was no shadow. He persisted, mumbling crazily. Eventually his perseverance was rewarded; as the sun began to move down, a shadow became visible. Good. But there was still the business about his feet. His feet faced the right way, but the prints he was leaving on the loose earth might be reversed. He took off his boots and stamped heavily. Then he stopped and walked back. Thank heaven, the prints faced the right way too. And his shadow was growing. Still not quite sure, he repeated his movements. The experiment became a dance as Munpa stomped along, turning around quickly every few yards.

Absorbed in his antics, Munpa didn't notice the Chinese gentleman who had been watching him closely. The spectator had been trying to draw Munpa's attention and now raised his voice.

"What are you doing there, good man?"

Munpa jumped up, suddenly transported from the eerie realm of the bardo to the everyday sphere of the living. A man had asked him a question. He studied the Chinese.

The gentleman was middle-aged, discreetly dressed in a gray robe of silk and a black waistcoat. His felt shoes were of good quality, and he wore an old-fashioned cap of black cloth. His expression resembled those of the smiling Buddhas in the caves.

Munpa thought that this Chinese could be a Buddha himself, descended to earth. He also looked a bit like the hochan in the traditional lama play.

The gentleman repeated his question. "What were you doing just now?"

"Oh . . . eh . . ."

The Chinese didn't insist.

"From what country are you?"

"Tsinghai."

"So you are a Tibetan. What brings you to Tun-huang? Do you live in this area now?"

"I came on a pilgrimage."

"All the way from Tsinghai? Perhaps you are engaged in some business?"

Munpa protested. "I'm not a merchant, I'm a lama."

The Chinese showed even more interest. "A lama? Where are you staying? Will you be here for a while?"

"I don't know. Right now I stay in one of those huts over there."

"You can stay at my house, if you like, for as long as you need to be here for your devotions. I'm also a follower of Buddha."

Munpa didn't understand. He was still trying to place the companion who had so suddenly materialized.

"You will be comfortable at my place, and I won't charge you anything. Be my guest. My house is close. You can see its roof next to those poplars. Please come. My name is Wang. Come whenever you please. The house is easy to find, but anybody will direct you should you get lost. I'm well known in the area."

Munpa still hesitated. There was no reason to disbelieve the polite gentleman, but was he *real*? Munpa didn't feel like plunging into another hallucination.

In the end he thanked Mr. Wang and accepted the invitation.

*

Wang didn't exaggerate when he claimed that everybody knew him. His very name was a password in northwestern China. Born into a wealthy and influential family that owned large estates and was part of the local government, he had pursued a life of ease and become a scholar, studying the philosophy of Confucius, gradually absorbing the established wisdom of a system that kept his country together for thousands of years. Encouraged by his parents, who were proud of their studious heir, he branched out into Taoism, specializing in the apparent contradiction between the teachings of Lao-tse and Confucius. Continuing his studies he came across Buddhism and his searching took a new turn. His introduction to the newer religion took the direction propagated by the meditation sect, called Ch'an in China and Zen in Japan.

The strict and disciplined method of Zen meditation finally transformed his mind. The present Mr. Wang was truly detached and peaceful. He no longer believed in good and bad and had lost his interest in politics. Is there such a thing as a *good* or *bad* government, he asked himself, considering the idea of wou wei or nonactivity originally suggested by Taoism and confirmed by Zen Buddhism. Things come about by the properties of their constituents, he told himself. Life and its components move along certain laws and it's useless to interfere with whatever goes on. He who thinks that he can direct a course of events fools himself, for he doesn't comprehend that he himself is part of the flow. The sage says that "he is immobile while he moves along, and acts while he does nothing."

Mr. Wang liked to quote both the founders of Taoism and the patriarchs of the Zen sect:

"I am on the bridge that crosses the current and wonder of wonders! It isn't the water that runs under the bridge but the bridge that moves on the water.

A cloud of dust comes from the ocean and the sound of waves is heard in the earth."

These statements refer to a perception differing from the limited view of the majority, for they find the black spot in a white field and the white spot in a black field or, as the Zen masters say, "the polar star in the southern sky."

Both schools of thought cultivate doubt, for things are not the way they seem at first glance. Whatever seems true harbors a lie, and the lie is a truth. Reality is equal to its exact opposite.

Mr. Wang had proved himself a diligent disciple of these ideas that lead to the peaceful smile of profound insight. He had become a sage himself, in the Chinese manner of "transcending the ten thousand things."

He didn't believe in making himself conspicuous. Having appointed an able cousin to look after his worldly affairs, and assured himself that his secretary contented himself with reasonable commissions, he used his wealth elegantly. Although he didn't spoil himself, he didn't criticize those who prefer to live in luxury and helped anyone who asked him for a favor, and also those who didn't ask but lived in needy circumstances. He lived simply without flaunting his austerities, married a lady of standing and owned only one concubine, a country girl whose poor father had been forced to offer her for sale. Buying the lovely girl for a good price had been both acceptable and profitable.

A similar attitude had prompted him to invite Munpa as a guest. Mr. Wang was not a sentimental man, so it wasn't charitable compassion that urged the deed. But here was this strange rustic, engaged in some weird dance, a man probably not right in the head. The man obviously needed help. Very well, Mr. Wang would help him.

Wang had never traveled but liked conversing with foreigners. They would teach him the ways of their countries, describe exotic landscapes and their cultures, provide all sorts of exciting details. A Tibetan, of the elevated rank of lama, would certainly be a worthwhile item in the Chinese's ever-shifting collection of knowledge.

Wang's house had been built in the local style and contained a number of pavilions separated by courts and surrounded by a high wall. Munpa wasn't lodged with the servants but was given a room in the compound where the secretary and his clerks lived. He was flattered by the honor and pleased to be introduced as a lama to Wang's dignitaries. The title of lama belied his appearance, for his robe was dirty again and more tattered than ever.

Another pavilion, decorated profusely and well furnished, housed Mrs. Wang and her chambermaids. The concubine had been assigned a smaller dwelling, where she lived with her little daughter and hoped to present her benefactor with a future son. A son would much improve the concubine's status, especially as Mrs. Wang already had two of her own.

Wang himself occupied the largest pavilion, where he lived alone with his books, surrounded on all sides by his family and employees. The entire household was run along strict and simple rules, as Wang would not permit any licentious behavior. Everyone was properly married, all children were expected to study under live-in teachers paid by Wang, and even the girls had their own, female, instructors.

Munpa was expected to restrain his movements within his own compound, but he felt the teeming activity of the other pavilions and was awed by his host's affluence. He wondered why Wang would be interested in a poor pilgrim met by chance on the road.

After a few days of rest and ample meals, Wang's secretary came to interview Munpa, asking questions about life in Tsinghai and noting the information with his brush, drawing meticulous characters on rice paper. These interviews became a daily routine, lasting for several weeks. Eventually the secretary seemed satisfied, enquiring after Munpa's health and presenting him with an excellent robe on behalf of Mr. Wang.

"He will see you tomorrow."

*

Munpa crossed the many courtyards. Wang welcomed his guest at the door of his splendid pavilion. "You have been of great use to me," he said formally, paying Munpa the compliment of choosing his words in such a fashion that host and guest were placed on a level of equality. "Now, venerable lama, I would like you to tell me about the way the clergy of Tibet practices its religion. What exactly is your belief?"

Munpa felt embarrassed. What did he know? As a simple trapa, with no more than the minimum of rustic schooling, his faith consisted of numerous disconnected items, many of them contradictory. He had never been able to formulate any coherent system of thought.

"I know little," Munpa confessed. "What could I say that would be of interest to a scholar such as yourself?"

Wang changed his approach. "Are there lama sages in Tsinghai? The abbot of your own temple, for instance?"

Munpa smiled when he thought of the old ignorant monk in charge of the little monastery in the Chang Tang. "No, but I was the attendant of a saintly guru."

"You were his disciple? Then he must surely have instructed you. And why do you speak in the past tense? Are you no longer the guru's disciple?"

Munpa, wishing that he could answer the question, remained silent. But he didn't want to be impolite to his amiable host. He thought he would try a question of his own.

"Do you believe, honorable Wang, that the Buddhas appearing in the murals of the caves are alive?"

It was Wang's turn to be muddled. There seemed to be no relation between this question and his own. Perplexed, he studied the anxious face of his guest. The poor fellow is deranged, Wang thought, remembering the way Munpa had danced on the bank of the river. He became concerned about Munpa's apparent insanity. He would have to go easily now and not upset the Tibetan.

"Well, that depends on what meaning we give to the expression 'being alive.' There are many different planes on which life manifests itself . . ."

He talks like the scholars, Munpa thought. I don't understand his theories, but there are different life planes, of course. The bardo, for instance. Once again he began to doubt his own existence.

"Honorable Wang, do you know perhaps if these Buddhas in the caves, and the Bodhisattvas who surround them, do not, every now and then, force whoever observes them to become part of their environment?"

Wang's confusion increased. He felt shaken, in spite of his customary equanimity. He had never heard such mad utterings before. Or was there some sense in this strange fellow's raving? Perhaps this matter of "being alive" was part of the religion of Tsinghai. It might be interesting to find out. Who knows, perhaps the lama had some exotic knowledge.

Patiently Wang started his interrogation again, careful not to contradict the lama. His gentle calm made Munpa believe he was once again faced by an advanced being, similar to the abbot of Supreme Serenity and the tao-che. The other two sages hadn't answered his questions either, not in a straightforward manner anyway.

Wang's tactics succeeded. Munpa was now ready to admit that the occult world didn't only exist, but that he, Munpa, had a way to enter it.

"If I question you about the Buddhas painted on the walls of the caves," Munpa explained, "you must understand that I have *seen* similar scenes, painted on other walls, that were alive and forced me to become part of them. I only managed to escape with great difficulty . . . and even now I'm not sure whether I really did escape."

Wang was listening intently. He regretted the absence of his secretary — all this should be written down at once. He didn't dare make notes himself, for any distraction could destroy his rapport with the lama. He phrased his questions with care. "Where were the murals that had tried to catch Munpa?" "Why had Munpa stayed at the monastery of Lanchou?"

Every answer that Munpa supplied led to a new question. Gradually all the facts came out. He told Wang about the miraculous turquoise, the murder, everything up to the nâga who returned the jewel and the demons who stole it again and left Munpa to hold a pebble.

The story took several hours, because Munpa didn't speak easily and Wang didn't interrupt when long pauses crept into the narrative. He noticed the lama's exhaustion and worried about the possibility of erratic behavior if he so much as hinted at any doubt regarding his unlikely tale.

"Very well. Why don't you return to your room now and rest awhile before dinner? What you just told me is most impressive."

Quite mad, Wang thought, as he said goodbye at the door. Poor fellow, the long pilgrimage has unnerved him of course. Must get him back to his own country; no doubt he will recover at home. There's a limit to what the foreign mind can absorb.

He waited a few days and then had the Tibetan shown

into his pavilion again. "Venerable sir," Wang said pleasantly, "to stay on in this country will not do you any good. You have met with demons, but they will leave you when you return to Tsinghai. Here you will find neither the turquoise nor its thief."

Wang hadn't believed Munpa and explained the entire adventure the lama had lived through as imagination. But Wang knew that all of life is imagination and that "reality" as we perceive it consists of multiformed projections of the mind. This knowledge made him sympathize with the unhappy lama, whom he would continue to help.

"You should be reassured at this point," he said, smiling at his attentive guest. "The demons who bothered you have no existence outside your own mind. If you pay them no attention, they will fade away by themselves. This is what the Buddha meant when he told us to liberate ourselves from a world where we force ourselves, through ignorance, to be born, to suffer, and to die."

Munpa nodded happily. "My teacher said the same: *They rise from the mind and extinguish themselves into the mind.*"

Wang approved. "Exactly! Remember that truth. Your adventures are no more than dreams. Do not allow them to trouble you.

"From here you can travel directly to Koko-nor, the great blue lake of Tsinghai, but the route is arduous and there are many mountain ranges to cross. A lone man will not easily survive the journey. You told me that you have a friend in Lan-chou, an innkeeper by the name of Chao. I advise you to go and see him and rest awhile before returning to your country. My secretary will see you soon and facilitate your journey."

Munpa never saw Mr. Wang again, but the secretary arrived the next morning, bringing another robe and a pair of good boots to replace the ones stolen by the border patrol.

Munpa's bag was filled with provisions, and he received a sizable sum in silver as well. Munpa had never been so rich in his life.

A servant brought a mule, accompanied Munpa as far as the An-hsi inn, and delivered a letter to its keeper. Wang wrote that the lama was to be given a good room and should join the first caravan to Lan-chou. The innkeeper was also instructed to make sure that the lama would be riding the entire distance.

So Munpa's journey reversed itself, considerably improved in quality. He traversed the desert again and suffered thirst and sand storms, but the small bag of silver clinking against his chest made it easy to ignore these temporary discomforts. The precious metal was a talisman too, different in quality from Odzer's glorious jewel, but it would buy its owner the necessities of life, and Munpa smiled as the dreary landscape glided past his trotting mule. No demons worried him now, and he forgot how he had gained and lost the turquoise. He was alive and well. The bardo episode had been no more than another painful illusion. Life did indeed consist of dreams. So said Mr. Wang. So said the lama teachers of Tibet.

*

The caravan reached Su-chou and Munpa stayed at the inn belonging to Nénuphar's brother-in-law. It was dark when he was shown his room, and when the innkeeper didn't recognize his guest Munpa didn't remind the man of their previous meeting. He left again before daybreak.

Within a few weeks, the caravan arrived at Lan-chou, the return journey completed without a single event worth noting.

7 WHEN HE HEARD that his travel companions would not be staying at Chao's inn, Munpa left the caravan at the outskirts of Lan-chou. He hailed two rickshaws, one for himself and one for his baggage, and gave the coolies Chao's address.

He had considered his future during the long journey. Honorable Wang had advised him to go home, and no doubt the counsel had been wise. But Munpa didn't feel the slightest desire to return to Tsinghai. Why? He wasn't too sure. All he knew was that the memory of the Chang Tang had begun to nauseate him. What would he do there? Live at the hermitage? But Gyalwai Odzer could not be served anymore. Munpa no longer wanted to think of the cave and the event that had led to his hasty departure. He had set himself a task then, he had tried to fulfill it, his plans miscarried. Perhaps he could try again, at some future date, when circumstances appeared to be favorable. Later, much later. Not now.

Now he would visit his good friend Chao

*

Chao happened to be in the court of his caravansary when Munpa's rickshaws arrived. Noticing the two vehicles and the visitor dressed in a resplendent Chinese robe, the inn-keeper bowed respectfully.

"Hello, old friend Chao!" Munpa shouted as he jumped down. "Will you put me up?"

Not all that much time had passed, but Chao needed a few moments before he could accept that this gentleman was indeed Munpa, the simple and savage Tibetan he had once employed as a stableboy.

"Do you have a room for me?"

Chao grinned. "Do you have to ask? Give me your baggage. You can have that room over there. It's the best I have available right now."

Munpa smiled too. The room was clean and comfortable, incomparable to the drafty lofts above the stables where he had slept before.

Facing each other over dinner that evening, the friends conversed.

"From where have you come?"

"From the Jade Gate of China," Munpa replied, hoping that Chao wouldn't know its location either and not pursue the subject. He was determined not to make a complete report on his journeys through the desert and to keep quiet about his relations with Nénuphar, the nâga who returned the jewel, and sage Wang. None of that connected with Chao's existence.

"Any news about the thief of the necklace?"

"What?" Munpa had forgotten the fabricated tale.

"The fellow who stole the necklace from the poor widow.'"

"Oh, him. No, no news."

"So he got away, the bastard."

"Yes. Whatever he got from selling the agates will be spent by now."

"And what did you do while you were away?"

"A little business," Munpa said modestly.

"You're rich now, aren't you?"

Munpa laughed. "Rich? No, not at all. I've saved a few coins, if that's what you mean. I didn't work for my own account, but I sold a bit here and there on commission."

"Any particular merchandise?"

Munpa lifted a leg, and the polished leather of his boot caught the light of the oil lamp. "Boots."

Chao slapped the table. "Boots from Sinkiang! Made by the Huie-Huie, right? Those Moslem fellows are very good at it. Was your boss a Huie-Huie too?"

"Yes."

"Did you bring any boots to sell here?"

Munpa shook his head. "No, I sold the entire stock out there. All I have for you is this small present."

He picked up the box he had been keeping by his side. Chao accepted respectfully. "Let's see what's inside."

Munpa grinned as the Chinese unpacked the four sweet cakes wrapped in paper, which he had bought when the caravan left An-hsi.

"Proof you have been in Sinkiang," Chao exclaimed. "I thank you. How nice of you to bring me these delicacies. But why didn't you stay when things were going so well for you?"

Munpa pulled a face. "I can't stand that country. Nothing but sand, not a blade of grass in sight, the water is bad and makes you sick. I've been ill many times."

"So you'll be going home to Tsinghai now?"

Munpa considered the question seriously. "No. Not for the time being. I would prefer to stay here."

"In my inn, I hope."

"Yes, but I'll pay you of course."

Chao raised his wine cup. "I'm happy to see that you did not return empty-handed, but please do not joke with me

114

about payment. You'll have your room and you'll be eating with me. Take your time and think about what you would like to do. In the meantime you can help me out if you like. I need a store man. There are so many goods coming and going that I can't keep track of them anymore. The stable-boys are overworked too. Perhaps you can give them a hand if you have nothing else to do. I'll be paying you a little wage while you're looking around."

Munpa accepted gladly and took up his duties the next morning. Time passed. Chao observed the ease with which Munpa dealt with people and thought of a possibility that might be profitable to himself and the Tibetan. He was overstocked with earthenware crockery and suggested that Munpa might sell the goods. Munpa left with a servant and three loaded mules, stayed away for two months, and returned with more silver than Chao had hoped for. The inn-keeper sent his assistant on another journey, to sell hats and boots this time, as well as a supply of lamb skins. On still another trip Munpa did a good business in rice and grains.

Chao was delighted and Munpa enjoyed his traveling, made in pleasant country and under favorable circumstances. On each return Chao would be waiting to celebrate another successful venture, and there would always be friends, such as the inn's regular guests and other acquaintances. As Munpa's mind opened to his new conditions, his intelligence developed and a flair for commerce, latent in all Tibetans, grew with it. He engaged in lengthy discussions with the passing merchants, learned details about the countries where they originated, and found ways of adapting his knowledge to the commerce that kept him busy.

His combined experiences changed his identity. He now found himself on the same social level as the merchants and no longer used the polite expressions he had been obliged to apply before whenever he came into contact with men who could claim a higher rank. Chao's respect, which dated from their very first meeting, also increased, and their mutual empathy gradually matured into genuine friendship.

As he adapted to his environment, Munpa took on Chinese ways. He still looked foreign, since he was taller in stature and darker of skin than the local population, but he now spoke fluent Chinese, no longer wore his robe of russet cotton, and even had his hair cut in the fashion of Lan-chou. He forgot that he had once been a miserable outcast, manhandled and jailed by ignorant constables, punished by a corrupt judge, and no one would ever remind him of that past misery, for the court of Lan-chou kept no records. He had been a wretch, punished by ten strokes of the bamboo and kicked back into the street. What would have happened to that despicable fellow? He would be dead now — starved to death probably, or with his throat cut in a drunken brawl. Who cares?

Years passed. Munpa didn't count them. The festivities of New Year repeated themselves three or four times. Life flowed on smoothly while Munpa, liberally rewarded by Chao, became a man of substance.

Munpa now owned a mule, a large strong animal purchased during a trip through Mongolia, when the beast was in poor condition and low in price. He had treated it well and the animal was worth a fair amount of silver now. Munpa also disposed of an excellent wardrobe, including a new robe lined with fur.

Chao, who wanted to include Tsinghai in the fast-growing territory where his goods were sold, was surprised to hear that Munpa would not travel in his own country. The ever-polite Chinese managed to forget his manners and insisted on being told the reason for this strange refusal. Munpa explained. He had been a trapa once, and monks are not allowed to live outside the territory controlled by their temples. If he returned to Tibet his superiors would be annoyed.

Chao pretended to accept what he believed to be a fabrication. Wasn't Munpa a free man now? An ex-monk is no longer a monk; Munpa had changed his status. Merchants can go where they like. Clever Chao respected Munpa's refusal to divulge his true reasons, however. The Tibetan was his friend and had proved himself to be a successful salesman. It would be unprofitable to delve too deeply into his past.

The wealthy innkeeper and entrepreneur had no sons and Chao's only daughter had married an official in the court of Lan-chou. The connection with the authorities of his city flattered Chao and he was pleased that his worthy son-in-law had made a lady out of his daughter. He accepted that the official was a gentleman and that his daughter could never return to the clamor of her father's courtyard and stables. But Munpa . . . well, there was still time.

Chao continued to study the Tibetan. Munpa kept on improving his position and became happier and more energetic in the process. He hardly ever thought of what he considered his remote past and had nearly achieved his attempt to forget the turquoise, the malicious jewel causing so many misfortunes. He almost blamed Gyalwai Odzer now for having been silly enough to have himself murdered, although he had never translated these feelings into words. The turquoise and the hermit had forced the course of Munpa's life into painful paths. Both teacher and talisman had refused to guide him during the quest. He didn't expect them to send him any signs now. He wanted to forget and go his own way.

*

But the "miracle," a result of Munpa's strong desire, would take place, although in a manner very different from his expectations.

One day, while traveling through the country, Munpa met a Mr. Teng, who happened to be staying at the same inn. Teng introduced himself as a dealer in wool and furs, also from Lan-chou, but at present visiting relatives. That evening the two men ate together and had a few drinks. The conversation became animated, they liked each other, and Teng invited Munpa to look him up when he returned to the city. Munpa remembered and paid a call on his newfound friend. A bottle of rice wine appeared as the two men renewed their contact.

"Really?" asked Teng. "You're a Tibetan? I would have taken you for a Mongolian. Weren't you talking that language to your servant when we met in the country?"

"Oh!" Munpa replied. "I speak some Mongolian too, but just a few words. I'm with the innkeeper Chao, and many of his guests come from that country. My servant is from there too."

Teng rubbed his chin. "A Tibetan. Amazing. From which part if I may ask?"

Munpa was embarrassed. He would have liked to say that he had been born in Lhasa or some other large Tibetan city, but he remembered that Chao knew that he was from Tsinghai. He might as well speak the truth, for if he boasted too much Teng might find out one day.

"I was born in the province of Tsinghai."

"No! Really? But that's quite a coincidence. My wife is from Tsinghai too! She will be happy to see a compatriot. She hasn't met any of her people since we married."

He got up and left the room. Munpa heard him call in the courtyard. "Tcham! Tcham!"

Munpa smiled. The honorable Teng was an affectionate husband. He was addressing his wife by the Tibetan courteous term meaning "elevated lady."

Teng returned, bringing his wife with him. She was obviously pregnant.

"How good of you to come." The woman was beaming broadly. "From what part of Tsinghai do you originate, sir?"

"From Aric."

"I was born in Tebgyai. We are both people of the plains."

"Indeed."

Teng laughed. "Neither of you look like nomads to me. You, sir, look Chinese now, and my wife wears the clothes of Lhasa. Well, why don't you excuse me for a while, I have things to do and it will be pleasant to speak your own language for a change."

He left the room and his wife smiled at Munpa. "He is such a good man. He does everything to make me happy. I will ask the cook to prepare a meal for three. I'll be right back."

Munpa sipped his drink. Amazing indeed. Many Tibetans marry Chinese, but it is unusual that a woman from the black tents of the herdsmen finds her way to a city like Lan-chou, at a considerable distance from the border.

When she came back, she asked the first question. "How long have you been here?"

"Oh, a long time already."

"And where do you live?"

"With the innkeeper Chao. I work for him. Your husband knows him well, because Mr. Chao is also a businessman. And yourself, when did you marry the honorable Teng?"

"Four years ago. I have a son, two years old now," she announced proudly.

"You'll soon have another. I congratulate you. Are you pleased to live in China?"

"Oh, yes. Lan-Chou is such a large and pleasurable city, so many people, so many new things to see each day, very different from living in tents and seeing nothing but yaks and sheep. And Mr. Teng is such a *good* man. I should be very grateful, and I am. He's rich too. He gives me anything I want; I don't even have to ask. And I don't have to work. There's a girl to help me with the housework, and there are two servants in the house and all the assistants that my husband employs in his business. The honorable Teng is a great gentleman." Tcham's eyes glistened with joy. She lives in heaven, Munpa thought. Good for her.

"Splendid, splendid," he said aloud. "But how did you manage to meet your husband?"

Her expression saddened. "That was a terrible time. We met in the Chang Tang. There were demons about. I'm so pleased to have escaped from there."

Munpa didn't like this sudden change in their conversation. He had had enough of demons. There was no need to meet with them again, even in retrospect. But the lady of the house was so happy to be able to speak her native dialect to someone who could understand her, and to discuss events that would be completely incomprehensible to any Chinese, even to her excellent husband, that Munpa had no choice but to listen to her story.

The description of the lady's early days didn't interest Munpa. He knew how the herdsmen live and their stories are all the same. That she married at age fifteen and that her first husband was old wasn't an unusual detail either. Munpa listened without paying much attention, saying the right things at the right times and hoping that the ordeal would soon be over.

"I was Kalzang's second wife," Mrs. Teng was saying, "and his first wife would beat me up cruelly. She liked hurting me. Her name was Tséringma. I used to be called Pasangma."

The names meant nothing to Munpa. He had known many females called Tséringma and Pasangma.

"Old Kalzang never protected me. Tséringma had given

him no children and I was supposed to have a son, but I didn't want to and I didn't become pregnant either."

There was a pause.

"And here I had a son within nine months, and the next one will surely be a son too."

Munpa nodded politely. "Surely."

"And then . . . and then . . . Lobsang saw me. One evening he came on his horse. I was herding Kalzang's sheep. He dismounted and then . . . it happened."

Munpa looked up when he heard her say "Lobsang" but lost interest again. There are hundreds of Lobsangs in Tsinghai, thousands perhaps. He understood what the lady meant by "it happened." *It* often happens in the highlands, like everywhere else.

"He came again, and asked me to run away with him, and I wanted to, of course. Old Kalzang was so rude, he smelled . . . Tséringma was treating me worse than ever. Lobsang said we would be rich. He was handsome too."

"What did he look like?" asked Munpa.

Mrs. Teng described her lover. Tall, but most herdsmen are over six feet. Wide-shouldered, vigorous. Nothing spectacular there either. Black hair. All Tibetans have black hair.

"We would have to leave at once, he said. He didn't want Kalzang to find us. We traveled all night, he and I on the same horse. It was a good horse, healthy and strong. Kalzang would never have found us. On that horse we were safe . . . such a nice horse . . . Oh! The poor animal!"

Munpa looked up. "Why do you say that? Did your lover ride it to death?"

"No, it wasn't that. I'll tell you. We could only travel by night and Lobsang was riding cross-country, because he was afraid he would meet people on the trails. I didn't agree, but he wouldn't listen. Kalzang's camp was a long way off already, and I was sure that the old fellow would be looking for me at my relatives' camp, which was north. We were riding south. I asked Lobsang where he was taking me and he became angry again. He behaved so strangely, sir. He said that demons were after us. We do have demons, you know. Some of them live in the lakes and others roam the plains. They hide in the cracks of the rocks, you know that, you're from there too."

Munpa nodded silently. He wished she would stop talking, but nothing could hold back Mrs. Teng now.

"Me, I never saw those demons, but Lobsang did. He heard them too. He would suddenly stop, jump off the horse, and stare about wildly, or he would put his hands behind his ears so that he could hear better and understand what they were saying to him. When we stopped to rest, he couldn't sleep or even lie down. He would sit for hours with his head hidden under his robe. And when I slept he would wake me up. "Can you hear them coming, Pasangma? Listen, they're talking to us. They're shrieking at me, Pasangma!" I couldn't stand it anymore, and his bad temper became unbearable. He was abusing me too. We were always by ourselves, because he still wouldn't follow the trails. By that time I began to doubt whether he knew where we were going. He had said that he wanted to go to Nepal, but did he have any idea where that country could be? There were no landmarks. How *could* he know?"

She sighed and clasped her hands. "And we were running out of food. We had some when we left, but we had been traveling for weeks and the saddlebags were getting empty. He sent me to camps, and hid himself and the horse, while I traded my bracelets for tsampa. We wouldn't sell the horse. He couldn't of course, we needed the animal. And I was too tired to walk by then. He had to let me ride while he walked next to the horse. Then I told him to sell the reliquary he carried under his robe. I had never seen it, but I knew it was there. To have a reliquary is nice, but one can do without, as long as the talisman is kept. I thought it might contain a little statue, or a mantra written on a bit of paper, or maybe a bit of cloth cut from some holy lama's robe."

She waited to see whether her visitor was following her story. Munpa nodded gloomily. "Please go on, Mrs. Teng."

"We had nothing left, you see. No tea, no butter, no tsampa, absolutely nothing. For three days we hadn't eaten. I had asked Lobsang before if he would sell the reliquary. Maybe it wouldn't be made of silver, but it had to have some value. The herdsmen at the next camp would give us food for it. What did the reliquary matter? He had told me we would be rich. Reliquaries could be bought in stores. We had to be going somewhere; there would be a city. But he always became angry when I mentioned selling the reliquary. I was so frightened of him; I didn't love him anymore. I would have run away if I had known where. Where could I have gone in the Chang Tang?

"But that night the hunger was tormenting us again. I saw him take the reliquary out of his robe. It had been sewn into cloth, so it would probably be made of silver after all. We would be able to eat at last! It was night, but I could see what he was doing by the light of the fire. Lobsang cut the cloth. He was trembling when he saw the reliquary slip out of its cover. Why? He wasn't doing anything wrong, was he? He opened its lid and took out a little parcel wrapped in blue silk. I wanted to see the talisman and crept closer to watch him unfold the silk. There was nothing in it. He picked up the reliquary again and felt inside it with the tip of his finger. Still nothing. And then he jumped up and yelled. He had said, a little before, that he had heard wolves howling and had tied the horse to a rock, but that terrible shriek frightened the animal and it broke loose and ran away. Lobsang cursed and ran after it. I was terrified.

I couldn't follow them. I can't run as fast as a man, and there were wolves. I hoped he might catch the horse and come back during the night. If he hadn't found it we could try together after daybreak. I picked up the reliquary. Fortunately it hadn't been damaged. I put it in the pocket of my robe. I sat by the fire all night. Lobsang didn't return . . ."

Mrs. Teng became silent.

Munpa understood. The report was clear enough. Lobsang, the thief-murderer. The reliquary that he wouldn't sell and that had been empty . . . *empty* . . .

He couldn't doubt the truth of what he had just been told. Every detail fitted exactly. And where would Lobsang be now? He had to force himself to speak in a normal voice.

"And then? At daybreak?"

"I looked at the reliquary. It had been made out of silver, with beautiful filigree on the back and front, decorated with golden lotus flowers. Each lotus held a pearl."

Munpa pressed his hands on the table. He had seen the reliquary once, held it in his hands when the hermit told him to repair its cover. But *empty?* And the supernatural jewel?

"Well . . . ?"

"I found Lobsang in the morning. Wolves had killed and eaten the horse. Lobsang had tried to defend it and the wolves attacked him too. When I came, the vultures had come already. Lobsang was dead too. I stumbled into his corpse."

Munpa was trembling and tried not to show his agitation by holding on to the table. He realized that he had to pretend curiosity if he didn't want to give himself away. "And yourself?"

"I don't know what happened afterward. The herdsmen said that they found me. They thought I was dead at first. I must have run away from that cursed spot, for they never saw the corpses or if they did they never talked to me about it. They put me on a mule and took me to their camp. I stayed with them for a long time. They looked after me when I was ill and took the reliquary as payment. When I recovered I had to work. It was the same life as at Kalzang's camp. Another old man said he wanted me. But then Mr. Teng came to buy wool, and put up his tent. I brought him hot water for his tea and he asked me if those people were my relatives. I said they weren't. We talked and then . . . it happened. After that I saw him often and when he was ready to leave he told me that he wanted to take me to China and marry me, because his wife had been ill and had died. I accepted his proposal and became happy. I'm still happy."

Munpa managed to congratulate Mrs. Teng on the fortunate outcome of her adventure. But she wasn't done yet.

"You don't look well. Did I upset you when I told you about the demons? I've always believed that the wolves that ate the horse and Lobsang weren't *real* wolves. Oh! Isn't it marvelous to be away from that land of demons and to live here in China?"

She looked at Munpa, who didn't reply. She seemed to feel sorry for deprecating her own country. "But in Tibet we have holy men too. You must have heard of the hermit Gyalwai Odzer, haven't you? He is famous all over Tsinghai."

Munpa struggled with an attack of vertigo.

"Have you?"

"Yes."

"Have you met him?"

"No."

"I haven't either, but I heard about the extraordinary happenings that took place in his cave. Some Tibetans talked about it to friends of Mr. Teng, in Hsi-nin. Maybe you heard too."

Munpa shook his head. "No, I have been away for a long time, trading in the country of the Huie-Huie."

"Well, I'll tell you what happened. Gyalwai Odzer

would sometimes meditate for long periods, for days or even weeks on end. When his door was locked nobody dared to disturb him. But when the cave stayed closed for as long as a month some of his disciples became anxious, especially as Odzer's attendant hadn't been seen for a long time either. They went into the hermitage and found the master's robes, sitting up by themselves on his meditation seat. There was no body inside the clothes. The two lamps on the altar were burning. On the floor, immediately in front of the seat, there was another robe belonging to the hermit's disciple-attendant. It had been spread out with the sleeves stretched to each side, and there was no body in that robe either. Have you ever heard such a miracle?"

"It happened before," Munpa whispered. "To Marpa, the teacher of Milarepa."

He wanted to say more, but his voice choked.

"Are you all right?"

He tried to shake his head. "I'm ill," he croaked, the words barely audible. "I will have to go home. I sometimes have attacks of fever . . . since I traveled in the country of the Huie-Huie. Please do not bother about dinner and tell your husband to excuse me."

"You're so pale. I'll tell the girl to call a rickshaw."

Mrs. Teng clapped her hands and gave the order. At that moment Mr. Teng's private rickshaw appeared in the courtyard.

"What happened?" Teng asked. "Aren't you staying for dinner?"

Munpa could only groan his excuses.

"The gentleman is ill," Mrs. Teng said kindly. "He suffers from the fever of the land of the Huie-Huie."

"It's true. You look terrible! You'll have to go to bed at once and colleague Chao can have a doctor called. I've heard about the Sinkiang fever. It attacks suddenly."

Munpa managed to get up and staggered about the room. Mr. Teng watched his guest anxiously. "I won't let you go alone. You're too ill. Tcham, I'll be back as soon as I can. Don't wait for me for dinner."

Munpa was helped into the rickshaw, which left at once, and Mr. Teng followed in another.

*

"Mr. Chao! Mr. Chao!" shouted Teng as the rickshaws entered the courtyard of the caravansary. The shouts conveyed such intense dismay that Chao came running out of the kitchen. He arrived as Teng was helping Munpa down, just in time to grab hold of his fainting friend. Together they carried the unconscious patient to his room.

The charitable Chao and one of his servants took turns watching the apparently lifeless body. Then Munpa stirred and became delirious and began to mumble the word *empty*, relating it to various objects.

"Empty . . . empty . . . Empty reliquary . . . Empty robes . . . Disappeared . . . Nothing . . . Empty . . . The wall . . . Entered into the wall . . ."

His hands fluttered, his face was flushed, and his eyes stared haggardly from deep sockets. Chao decided to call a doctor. But what sort of doctor? The innkeeper's ideas about medicine were fairly modern, and he remembered the proximity of a hospital run by American missionaries.

Within minutes he was explaining that the patient was too sick to be moved and that he wanted the doctor to come over to his inn, adding that both he and the patient would be able to pay in cash, both for the visit and any future treatment.

To be able to pay is always a good recommendation. One of the foreign doctors accompanied Chao, saw Munpa, and stated that the patient was in critical condition, diagnosing brain fever, a term Chao didn't understand. The doctor suggested intensive care and had Munpa carried to the hospital on a stretcher. Chao went too and insisted that Munpa be given a private room. He paid in advance, negotiated that he alone would be allowed to visit the patient, and went back to get some rest.

The doctor did his best, assisted by the hospital's trained staff, and Munpa's sturdy body responded to the remedies. But six weeks went by before he could remember what had happened and regain sufficient strength to be able to walk in the hospital's garden.

Sitting in the shadow of ornamental trees and surrounded by flowers, Munpa felt as if he had just been born and that the Munpa just before the illness hadn't been more than some animated figment of a dream or a barely remembered previous incarnation, entirely different from the actuality of this recovering Chinese merchant enjoying the sun at the hospital of Lan-chou.

This other Munpa, Munpa Des-song, was dead, or, rather, had transformed his body into thin air. The fact was obvious. People had *seen*, even *touched* the empty robe prostrating itself in front of Gyalwai Odzer's seat. A miracle performed by the hermit. Munpa accepted the manifestation as such. He remembered having bound Odzer's body with cords, offering some food on the dishes of the altar, lighting the two lamps, the lamps that burned on for months. The miracle would have happened after he had run from the cave. The hermit, not dead at all, only showing the exterior signs of death, would have caused the disappearance of his body, as Marpa and other great teachers had done before him. But what about Munpa? He had prostrated himself, but afterward he left. He was quite sure of the fact. He had traveled in Tibet, China, Sinkiang, had crossed and recrossed the desert, been Nénuphar's lover, honorable Wang's guest, Chao's friend — good old Chao who had visited him only the day before — and now he was a merchant sitting on a bamboo seat in a garden belonging to a hospital run by blue-eyed demons who weren't demons after all but Americans, people from a country near the edge of the world. So? What was he to think of that empty robe that looked like the one he had been wearing when he left the hermitage?

And the empty reliquary? The turquoise that wasn't there? Had it been taken away? By whom? Certainly not by Lobsang, for Mrs. Teng couldn't have been lying. Her story had to be genuine. Lobsang believed in the existence of the jewel; the care with which the murderous thief had unfolded the strip of silk proved his faith. So was the reliquary already empty when Lobsang tore it from the neck of the hermit? Had the turquoise *ever* existed outside the imagination of the gurus and magicians who transmitted it down their venerable lineage, who believed to be handing over something, a power incorporated in the jewel, and who passed on nothing but emptiness?

Emptiness. It had been efficient. It had touched the sick of Tsinghai and cured them; others had become healthy by merely invoking the image of the turquoise. Manipulating the nonexistent turquoise had brought rain, green fields, fodder for the animals, food for the humans.

Lobsang had killed because of this jewel that didn't exist, and had been killed in turn by demons who pursued him relentlessly through the Chang Tang.

The nonexistent turquoise had forced Munpa to leave his country to catch the fleeing Lobsang and eventually changed him into this Chinese merchant who would never again take care of a hermit in the highlands.

All this activity caused by nothingness, by the power of that-which-is-empty.

He saw the little people populating the walls of the

Zen temple of Supreme Serenity. Phantoms. "They didn't have to draw me into their play," he mumbled. "I *am* in it, *everything* is. *The world is no more than a play of images, superimposed on emptiness.* Who said that? Mr. Wang? The tao-che? The abbot of the Zen monastery? . . . I don't know anymore."

Munpa's head dropped with sleep. A nurse came to fetch him.

"Please go inside. The sun is going down, and it will be too cold for you here."

Munpa rose obediently. He wanted to sleep again. The next day he felt rested and peaceful.

"You're looking well," the doctor assured him. "You can leave whenever you like. A bit of distraction is what you need now. Look up some friends, enjoy yourself for a while. Some tremendous shock must have caused the illness you have now recovered from. Whatever it was, try to forget it. Think ahead. You're still young."

Munpa believed him. He felt very young. Hadn't he just been born again?

A message was sent to Chao, who came to fetch his friend.

"All you need is some good food," Chao said happily. "Just give me a few weeks and we'll make you as strong as you used to be. The doctor says you're doing very well and has predicted a complete recovery. You've been really ill, you know! Sinkiang has been a bad place for you, it gave you the fever and allowed that miserable thief to get away."

"I found him," Munpa said quietly.

"How? You said you hadn't!"

"I have found him since then."

"Here? Where is he?"

"He is dead."

"Dead? And what happened to the necklace?"

"He is dead," Munpa repeated.

"What? The necklace is dead?"

"Everything is dead. Nothing exists, nothing but phantoms, moving about by the power of nothingness."

Chao nodded pleasantly. The doctor had said that Munpa might still behave somewhat irrationally and had urged Chao not to contradict the patient should he show any signs of abnormal behavior.

"Right," Chao said. "It's getting late. Why don't you rest awhile?"

Munpa smiled and closed his eyes.

*

When he woke the sun had just reached the wall opposite his khang. He rested his eyes on its blank, whitewashed surface. A servant came in to bring him his breakfast, and a little later Chao paid a brief visit to his friend. Munpa got up, walked about a little, and climbed back on the khang. The day passed, followed by others that were as restful and pleasant as the first. Munpa remained quiet and pensive while he took part in a secret dialogue that flowed on gently and didn't demand his full attention. Gradually he began to pay attention to what was going on in the caravansary. Soon he was working again, and discussing business with Chao over dinner, displaying an intelligence and practical sense that amazed the Chinese.

Our savage from across the border is certainly an astute businessman, Chao thought, observing his friend closely. Then it was Chao's turn to reflect, but on a subject totally unlike the cause of Munpa's pondering.

Chao had been informed that the associate who ran his branch office in Urga had died. The man left a wife and several small children and the widow wanted to return to Lan-chou to live with her relatives. In Urga matters were temporarily directed by the chief clerk, a Mongolian with some business experience but not sufficiently gifted to arrange large transactions. Chao thought of Munpa, who could easily handle the business and whose honesty had been proved on many occasions. It was true that Munpa was a foreigner, but he was born in Tsinghai, a province under nominal Chinese control, and could therefore be considered somewhat Chinese too, more Chinese than the free Mongolians could ever be. Chao was pleased by his own childish reasoning, although he knew that the argument was superfluous. Wasn't Munpa his true friend? I will offer the vacancy to Munpa, Chao decided, but I'll wait until I'm sure that he has completely recovered.

Matters came to a head fairly quickly. An Urga-bound caravan arrived at the inn, and its merchants worried about not having sufficient merchandise to load their many camels. Chao saw an opportunity to send more goods to his branch office, but didn't want to trust the Mongolians with his valuable wares. He took Munpa aside, explained the situation, and offered to make the Tibetan his full associate.

Munpa immediately agreed to the transfer.

"Are you sure that your health has returned?"

"Absolutely, friend Chao."

"Good. The caravan will be leaving soon. You'll be accompanied by two of our servants, and I'll select a couple of good mules so that you can ride them in turn."

The merchants still had business to attend to in Lanchou so Munpa had ample time to prepare for his departure. He was looking forward to the new venture.

＊

When, just after daybreak, the large Mongolian camels began to file out of the caravansary's courtyard, Munpa and Chao waited at the gate. There was no hurry, as it would take a while for the camels to find the easy rhythm that habitually carried them through the great desert, and Munpa's fast mule would easily catch up with them.

Munpa jumped into the saddle and smiled at Chao. He knew how much he owed the innkeeper who had assisted in his transformation from rustic herdsman to educated merchant, now on his way to a nonexisting goal.

"Thanks for everything, Chao. You have been a father to me. Please don't worry. I'll be taking good care of your interests out there. You won't be sorry that you sent me."

Chao returned the smile. Neither could think of anything more to say. Munpa's whip touched the mule's flank and the animal trotted off, eager to join its companions.

*

A whiff of dry wind hit the rider's face, stinging his cheeks with a few particles of sharp sand, the sand of the desert. Munpa shrugged. He no longer cared about the Gobi's terrors and the storms, mirages, and demons that would be waiting for him. He no longer cared about anything. The abyss of his mind had swallowed all the images of his past, even the most sacred: that of the teacher whom he had left, wrapped in a monastic robe, seated on cushions, the guru whose corpse had evaporated so mysteriously. Hadn't the former Munpa, sworn to return Odzer's life together with the turquoise that never was, evaporated as well? That Munpa was gone forever — only the disciple's empty robe was left behind. This new Munpa, riding a mule to Urga, could not be the other, the trapa of the poor little Tsinghai monastery, the fellow who had wanted to chase a shadow.

Shadows and phantoms, the beings and things of this life had so been described to him. The sages who talked that way were undoubtedly right. It was neither necessary to equal their wisdom nor to contradict it.

He was no more than a small insignificant shadow, dressed up like a merchant, moved by a power emanating from a nothingness, a nonexisting turquoise. But this particular phantom wanted to live, to complete its dream merchant's act.

Munpa cracked his whip and set out happily for Mongolia to paint the images of his new career on the transparent backdrop of the Great Emptiness.

The Power of Nothingness has been set
in linotype Granjon, designed in 1924 by the
English printer George W. Jones. It is based on the
letterforms of Claude Garamond, a sixteenth-century French
punchcutter and typefounder, and named for Robert Granjon,
a French designer of the same period.

*

Composition is by Lamb's Printing Company.